Sarah Stuart Robbins

Tony Starr's Legacy

SALZWASSER
VERLAG

Sarah Stuart Robbins

Tony Starr's Legacy

Reprint of the original, first published in 1863.

1st Edition 2022 | ISBN: 978-3-37500-325-8

Verlag (Publisher): Salzwasser Verlag GmbH, Zeilweg 44, 60439 Frankfurt, Deutschland
Vertretungsberechtigt (Authorized to represent): E. Roepke, Zeilweg 44, 60439 Frankfurt, Deutschland
Druck (Print): Books on Demand GmbH, In de Tarpen 42, 22848 Norderstedt, Deutschland

TONY STARR'S LEGACY:

OR,

Trust in a Covenant-Keeping God.

BY THE

AUTHOR OF "WIN AND WEAR."

NEW YORK

1868.

TONY AT HIS MOTHER'S GRAVE.

[FRONTISPIECE

CONTENTS.

TONY STARR'S LEGACY.

I.

The Maiden Aunts.

JUST at the north side of the Methodist meeting-house, in the pretty village of Mountford, stands a neat white cottage. It is only a story and a half high, but no one passes it without feeling how complete it is. It has four small windows, with green blinds, and a green door in front. Every body knows who lives there; so there is no need of putting over the door the sign, S. & R. Denton, Dressmakers. The "oldest inhabitant" could not remember when they came to town, nor had any one ever heard them called any thing but Aunt Cily and Aunt Roxy. It is a question whether they remembered themselves.

that they had been baptized Silence and Roxana, or would either of them have answered to the more dignified name of Miss Denton?

Aunt Cily was the oldest, though this could not be gathered from her looks, for as far as the impression Time had made upon them, he seemed to have dealt very impartially, and to have treated them both alike. They had supported themselves for so many years as village dressmakers, by the patient and very industrious use of their needles, that they came to have a kind of personal resemblance to them.

They were one size all the way down from their shoulders to their feet, and straight and stiff as the steel itself. They always had a shining, clean look, too, as if they had been worn and rubbed until they were in a high state of polish.

One look at them would assure you that a young dressmaker, even with the "newest fashions direct from Paris," had a very poor chance in competition with them. They had an "inalienable right," and were as much a part of a wedding or funeral as the parties most immediately concerned. Their lives were thus interwoven with the lives of every family in Mountford—very humbly and unpretendingly, but none the less surely for that. Not a path to any house in the village was better worn than that leading to their front door; so they nailed creeping roses where others might have placed a sign, plaiting them firmly on to the house with trimmings of woodbine, and planting a gessamine by way of tassel, with its purple, drooping flower and coral button when the flower is set. If these were all so prim, precise and neat, that not a leaf or a bud dared show itself but where it was sure it would find an exact match, it only told an observer what was to be expected from the work done within; it was better than a newspaper column of advertisements.

In one window stood always, summer and winter, a few house plants, and what struck those who were familiar with the culture of flowers as very singular, was the fact, that in all seasons they looked precisely the same, never any taller or shorter, broader or narrower, never with a yellow leaf, and never with any that were very green. It was as if they had imbibed the spirit of the house, and could only live and thrive in this particular way. The Hydrangea was the only one that ever ventured to show any freaks, and these the ever-watching eyes and scissors soon restored to the perfect state. Nothing ever could change, or at least nothing which it was in their power to prevent. The common ravages of Time they met and repaired as soon as visible, and in their own personal appearance and dress they were rigidly alike, and as far as they could be, unchangeable. They wore the same caps over hair equally blanched; trained their two little "wintry" curls over a similar number of wrinkles in their pale cheeks; put on steel-bowed spectacles the same year, of the same power, over eyes which, however, nature by some mistake had failed to make alike,—for Aunt

Cily's were of that peculiar brown hue which never fades, and never shows that it has grown dim, while Aunt Roxy's were blue—faded blue—almost a weak gray, only there was something behind them which would not fade, but would look out of them bright and clear and sky-like, in expression if not shade. Indeed, if you very closely examined the two faces, you could see that when they were younger there was no difficulty in telling them apart, for Aunt Cily had a long nose, without so much as a crook or a bunch, and Aunt Roxy's was decidedly Roman, and rather large for that. For their mouths,—there the resemblance grew very striking again, and why shouldn't it? these sisters had never expressed a different sentiment for forty long years that any one had heard, and their mouths, from using the same forms of speech, would naturally grow alike.

In their dress, too, they were punctilious in their intention of making it precisely the same. Neat chocolate prints for every day wear, fitting to their needle figures without wrinkle, seam, or any such blemish; gray silks, with black trimmings, for Sunday wear, with the gray straw bonnets, "done over and over and over," until very little of the originals remain; a large gray blanket shawl in winter, a thin gray merino one in summer, and their change of wardrobe was all told. The great wonder to any one, who took the trouble to wonder about it at all, was, how they ever knew the difference between their various articles of dress themselves, and why Miss Cily was not always wearing Miss Roxy's things, and Miss Roxy Miss Cily's.

They, both of them, attended the Methodist church hard by which they lived, and they were active, zealous sisters; the main dependence for every good word and work of the various pastors under whose ministrations they sat. Always punctual, rain, snow, sleet or sunshine, at every meeting, always in their place in Sabbath-school, and always, strange as it may seem, able to command classes of the most intelligence and value.

It must not be supposed because they were dressmakers, and sewed almost all their time, that they neglected their own education ; far from it, when they worked at home, which was the greater part of the time, one read, unless the work was very pressing, while the other sewed, and in this way they managed not only to keep up with the leading events of their own day, but they had a good deal of what the country folks called "larning," and they knew how to make proper use of it. It was quite a holiday in any of the families where they worked if they could be persuaded to come, one or both, to them instead of taking the work home, for they were always so pleasant, and always "knew every thing that was going," though they repeated the news in a kind of colporteur manner, taking away every possible sting, harm, or ill-feeling, and leaving only what was good and would do good.

You may be sure, that loved and respected as the maiden sisters were away from home, they must have been very happy and contented when there; for after all, say and do what we will, for appearance, that great judge—"*every body*" is pretty clear-sighted, and the way Mrs. Jones and Deacon Brown and Sam Caxton speaks of you, if not just as you *seem* abroad, is very apt to be just as you *are* at home. Home, then, was a pleasant place to our old aunts; a quiet, sunny, cheerful, prayerful little nook, neat and clean, as if it had been purified and set apart for a sacred purpose; and so it had. It was set apart to live a useful, holy life in, and they loved to hang about it small tasteful things peculiar to them, but offered with something of the same spirit with which devotees in Catholic countries hang what they call "votive offerings" around the shrine of their chosen saints. In truth, this small, white cottage was their shrine; but they did not worship it,—only in and around it. They covered its parlor floor with a bright rag-carpet, very crooked, but still intensely regular in its pattern; hung large lithograph pictures of the

"Lord's Supper," "Jesus blessing little children," "Christ raising the widow's son," and the "Madonna," with the holy infant in her arms, in neat black frames, on the walls; put in it six wooden chairs, a table with a Bible and Hymn-book, and two foot-stools, one with a dog wrought in old-fashioned sampler-stitch by Aunt Cily, and the other, a cat, done in a similar way by Aunt Roxy. The dog always had his face turned in most amiable proximity to the cat, and for the matter of a growl, or a quarrel taking place between them, their very faces denied any such wish even if the good aunts would have allowed it. A small, neat bedroom led off from this into which they always put the stray minister or agent, who dropped in to spend the night. It was a kind of "prophet's room," and the aunts looked into it daily, to see if it was in perfect order, with a kind of veneration.

Another room, on the other side of the front door, was the sitting and working room, without any carpet, but with its pictures of Whitfield, and Wesley, and Olin, in mahogany frames, on the neat white-washed walls. From this, opened out their bedroom and their kitchen; so scrupulously clean were both apartments that, as Mrs. Dodge, the greatest sloven in the parish used to say, "it made one feel as if they could eat off from any part of them."

"Cleanliness," clearly in their estimation, was "next to godliness," and this not only in-door, but out of door neatness. It almost seemed as if the wind, frolicking however merrily it might be with the stray straws and leaves, never deposited one any where in the sacred precincts of the old sisters' yard, or little garden plot. No dog thought of laying down the well-gnawed bone, even behind the back door; and if a cat had caught a mouse on the premises, she would certainly have stolen off to some remote hiding place before she ventured to eat it.

It was remarkable, but the sisters did not tolerate any live thing, but themselves, within or without the house. There had been times, when they had tried to domesticate a cat, but the first accident that happened to her always brought about her dismissal without any delay; and as for chickens, they would have foregone the luxury of eggs for their whole lives without a complaint, rather than have kept them.

There were, however, some of the summer visitors, whom they invited, and further still, set traps to entice; those were the birds and the bees.

Aunt Cily always put out the crumbs upon the door steps as soon as the first bird made its appearance, and Aunt Roxy obtained the sweetest, most honey-dewed flowers, to tempt the bees.

We have been thus particular in our description of the maiden aunts, because they are very important personages in our history of "Tony Starr's Legacy," and we wish the reader to become well acquainted with them. Our story now leads us to the sitting room, one cool fall evening, just when they began to make a little fire on the bright "brass dogs," in order to have the cheerfulness, perhaps more than the warmth of the blazing wood, and, indeed, it is very cheerful. The sparks leap up out of the clear flames, like frolicking children, and chase one another round and round the ample fire-place, until in very exuberance of their joy, they fly up the broad chimney and are lost to sight. And then the ruddy fire-light lays itself on the faces of the good dead men that are hanging on the walls, with a kind of life-giving power. Whitfield almost smiled as if he were still speaking those "glad tidings of great joy." Wesley seemed rejoicing that though dead, he was still living in the affections and life of so many followers ; and, not only the pictures caught and gave back the cheerful home light, but the very grains of sand, imprisoned on the spotless floor, sparkled and glowed like little gems, as they were,—but not gems of worldly value,—only of the true, pure gems of a well ordered house.

The small round table, was drawn before the fire-place, to the precise spot it had occupied for so many years; the identical small solar lamp was burning on the exact centre of the table; the two low rocking-chairs, were uttering the monotonous "click" with which they always announce the reflective moods of the sisters; and the sisters themselves, were sitting in them with expressions of face very similar, and not at all in accordance with the appearance of every thing else in the room. They were not only sober, but they were positively sad, and withal, very much troubled. Between them, on the table, lay an open letter, to which they both cast sidelong glances, every now and then, as if that had been the occasion of their perplexity, as, indeed, it was.

For a long time they both sat silent, with their eyes fixed steadily on the fire. At last Aunt Roxy said, with something very like a groan—

"And of a galloping consumption, too."

"Yes, a galloping consumption," repeated Aunt Cily. "You know her father died of it, and her mother would have, if she hadn't gone off with a fever just before. Cynthia never was like the rest of us. I mind, when our mother used to say, she would come to a different end from any other of her children; and so she has, sure enough. Who would have thought it? and now her daughter, Mary Ann, is to come back from way off there, where she went, in a galloping consumption."

"But the baby, only to think of that," said Aunt Roxy, as lost in wonder; Aunt Cily had seemed unable to proceed. "Only to think of that, a baby to come to—"

"And a boy, of all things," said Aunt Cily, while a real shudder ran over her frame. "A great, noisy, tearing, swearing, wicked boy!"

"It is only a baby now, you know."

"That is all the worse; a baby, of every thing, to come into this house," and Aunt Cily cast a disconsolate look around the apartment, as if she was taking her farewell of every earthly joy.

"And Mary Ann in a galloping consumption!

Let us see, what is it the minister writes?" and Aunt Roxy unfolded the letter and read—

"DEAR SISTERS IN CHRIST:

"I am an entire stranger to you, and feel much delicacy in communicating the sad intelligence, which, as present pastor here, I feel it my duty to write. You will be, I hope, prepared to receive it, with much Christian resignation, knowing that whom our heavenly Father loveth, he chasteneth.

"Mrs. Starr is a member of my parish, and informs me she is your niece, the only remaining child of your sister, Mrs. Cynthia Doane. Mrs. Starr was married two years ago to a young lawyer of this place, who died four months since of typhoid fever. Soon after his death Mrs. Starr became the mother of a little boy; but, since her sickness, she has given every indication of having fallen into a rapid decline, and as she is left without means, she expresses an earnest desire to return to Mountford, and place her child under your care before her death. I understand, from her, that you are the only relatives she has living, and I have no doubt her appeal to you for sympathy and help, will but verify the truth which our Lord gives us, as one by which we may test our fitness for his everlasting kingdom—our willingness to feed his lambs. Mrs. Starr will leave for Mountford in a few days, as I have procured safe company for her, and in her state of health there is no time to be lost.

"Hoping the blessed Saviour, who went about doing good, comforting the sick and afflicted, and caring for those who had no one else to care for them, will give you largely of His Spirit, and so enable you to receive and comfort this stricken one, that you so may merit the plaudit, 'Well done, good and faithful.'

"I remain, yours truly,

"NORTON COBB."

Aunt Cily's eyes were overflowing with tears when the letter was finished.

"Poor child, poor child!" she said. "I dare say it came proper hard on her, and that young baby, too. Four months old, only think of that Roxy, with its colics and its nus bottle, and its being trotted to sleep time after time."

"Feed my lambs," said Aunt Roxy, without apparently being very conscious what words she was uttering; her thoughts were evidently more with the colic and the nus bottle and the trotting.

"If it had only been a girl, now, how much more like 'a lamb' it would have been," and Aunt Cily's voice showed that the verse, if it had been unconsciously repeated, had touched her.

"Mary Ann, perhaps, will be the lamb!"

"I wonder now, if she is a member of the church, Mr. —— what-is-his-name, there, don't say one syllable about it; I am afraid she is not; and in a consumption, too, its dreadful—dreadful!"

"Dreadful!" echoed Aunt Roxy. "A very rapid decline, and he don't say no more what the baby's name is. Now, I hope she has had the sense to give it some good Scripture name, —our father's, say. Why, there is something reminds one of the Bible in its very sound— "Isaac—Isaac Starr."

The walls of the still room seem to echo the new name, with a kind of start, as if its very first sound had disturbed its quietude, with a foreboding of its future.

"But a boy, any how, even if its name *was* Isaac. Sister—sister Roxy, what can we do?"

"Well," said Roxy, giving a little fidgety start, as if groaning over it was not going to help them out; "when we had Laura Jane's wedding outfit, with all its silks and satins, to get done in a month, I remember we sat and were just as knocked up as we are now; but after all, it was only taking our thimbles and our needles, and our thread, and our scissors, and putting a little zest to them, and the work was done. So now, if we go to it in real earnest, I dare say we shall find"—and Aunt Roxy's voice had a droll sound, as if she was frightened at the words she was uttering—" even a cradle for the baby."

" And where shall it stand ?"

" Oh, yes, sure enough, where ?" and a very blank look of dismay spread over both faces, succeeded by a dead silence.

" There won't be any use," said Aunt Cily, first interrupting it, " in our having them in here, 'cause babies get pins in their mouths, and sometimes choke to death."

" And then," continued Aunt Roxy," if she is in a decline, that best carpet of ours would be all tatters, with so many feet pattering round upon it."

" And the boy, too !"

" Yes, the boy, too. If it only had been a girl she would not tear over it so like a great, thumping boy, with cow-hide boots."

" But Mary Ann must have the prophet's room for all that, and—yes—I guess, that's it," and Aunt Cily's face caught the bright blaze which suddenly sprung up from the fire, or else reflected the warmth and brightness of her heart, I cannot say which. "She *shall* have the prophet's chamber, and a nice little stove put up in the parlor, and we will 'feed our lamb,' so that our Great Shepherd can say, 'Well done good and faithful.'"

Here Aunt Cily broke down with a feeble sob, which was returned from the opposite side of the table, and a choked voice said, "Yes, we will feed the lambs."

II.

Preparations.

IT was quite a disappointment to the maiden aunts, when they began early the next morning to prepare their parlor for their expected guests, that they could find nothing to clean. Every part of the room was so spotless, so delicately nice, that the most fastidious eyes, which were those of Aunt Roxy, with her new spectacles on, could find nothing to do. To be sure, the workman in putting up the stove, made a very little dust, but it was so soon removed; really it was nothing in comparison to the great wish, which they had, to do something for "the Lamb."

Every day, for the next week, before the arrival of the stage which came from "York State," and, consequently, brought the Western travellers, a fire was put into the new stove ; the whitest of beds turned down, to insure a thorough airing, and fresh chrysanthemums added to the two old-fashioned pint tumblers, which, from time immemorial, had been made on all state occasions to take the places of vases. There was a brilliant show. Aunt Cily had not hesitated to pick the very choicest for "the Lamb ;" and here they were, of every color and every grade of doubleness. White, purple, red, blue, straw color, and all so fresh, that they fairly loaded the parlor with their heavy perfume ; and had they been anything but flowers, and those, too, which were the pride and glory of the garden, they would soon have been banished as "too strong." But here they were, the tumblers, from their daily accessions, quite filled, and each separate flowers, standing stiff and prim as a soldier on drill.

Every thing was ready but the cradle. To be sure, Aunt Roxy, after dark one night, had made a stolen visit to old Mrs. Ware, to inquire where such an article might be obtained, if needed ; but she made it with very much the same guilty feeling with which a young girl inquires at the Post-office for her first love letter. She was afraid people would laugh at the idea of an old maid wanting to borrow a cradle. And now we come to a fault in both our good sisters, which we would very willingly have concealed, if the truth would have allowed—their one weak point was, the fear of being laughed at. No one could have told, indeed they never knew themselves, how they became so sensitive here ; but so it was, and so it happened, that, with every other preparation perfectly attended to, this one point of the cradle was neglected ; for Mrs. Ware had long since parted with hers for some of the grandchildren, and having lost the run of the babies in the village, could afford them no assistance. They spent a great many hours trying to devise a substitute. They took, at last, the large willow basket, which bent over at the sides, not unlike a modern straw cradle, and tied it on to the seat of an old wicker-bottomed rocking-chair, whose back had been years before broken off, and then, after a whole evening's work, they made it, the cunningest, nicest little affair of a cradle in all Mountford.

The old ladies placed it between them, with great satisfaction. Sometimes Aunt Roxy's foot rested on the rocker, catching the mother's motion as truly as if it had lulled to sleep a whole generation of babies; and then Aunt Cily would start it with a counter motion, and sometimes they would both put their feet on together, and so unconsciously hold it quite still.

It was very plain, that though that basket had been filled with nothing but rolls of cloth of every shape and size for fifty years, it had come, in its owners' estimation, to its true destiny now. It had been clumsy and rather in the way as a work basket; it was admirable, and could always find a place as a cradle, though it was destined to hold a boy. On the fifth day after the arrival of the letter, the sisters refused a most lucrative piece of work; they were otherwise engaged, they were going to make an outfit for the cradle; so they locked their two outside doors, dropped the shades over the windows in the sitting-room, and with very nimble fingers commenced their task. First the small feather bed, then the little cotton mattrass, the tiny pillow, and the smooth, white sheets, two darling blankets made of the soft homespun flannel their mother wove, and then the real silk bed-quilt, the result of the bits of silk from every dress they had made since their busy trade first begun. This same silk patch, which had been designed for an easy-chair, a couch, two ottomans, any thing and every thing but a cradle-quilt. But there it was; and when the preparations were all complete, it was as good as a first-rate picture to see how these two old aunts admired it, how they turned the cradle this way and that, and looked at it in every imaginable light and position; how they spread it over the edges of the the basket, until it concealed the rockers themselves, and then tucked it in with the look of a French bed-covering; and then how, when in the midst of their admiration and experiments they were startled by a loud knock at the door, they hurried it off into the bed-room. With nervous impatience and much real trepidation, they allowed the knock to be repeated over and over again, until the cradle was thoroughly concealed and the bed-room door close locked upon it. Then Aunt Cily approaching the window, lifted a corner of the shade, and and peeped out.

"Why, Roxy!" she exclaimed, in much alarm, "if here it aint come; Mary Ann, stage, baby and all, and I dare say the fire in the parlor has burned down too."

She immediately opened the door and stood there, while the busy driver, having knocked, as he said, "times, and loud enough to wake the dead," was busy unstrapping the small black trunk, and lifting out from under a huge quantity of luggage a medium sized carpet-bag. This done, he opened the stage door for a man who

TONY'S FIRST APPEARANCE.

had been impatiently watching him, and out he sprang, reaching back for a moment to take something with him, which Aunt Cily saw, from its uncouth form, could be nothing but a baby.

"Miss Denton," he said, as he came to her with the bundle, "I suppose. This is Mrs. Starr's little boy." He held the baby toward her, evidently expecting her to take it, but the thought never occurred to Aunt Cily. She only moved away that he might go into the house, and evidently had a sort of dim thought of the cradle.

The man next encountered Aunt Roxy, to whom, without any further ceremony, he handed the child, and went back to the stage. By this time Aunt Cily had recovered sufficiently from her surprise, to go towards the gate and welcome the sick niece. Poor, frail thing; Aunt Cily saw, from her first glance at her, that the minister was right. She was in a rapid decline. Why, she did not look able to step on her own feet. So Aunt Cily, with a little more alacrity than she had shown towards the baby, opened her strong arms, and almost lifted the tired mother in, saying as she did so, in a voice neither dry nor sharp, as her appearance had led the man to expect, but soft and really tender,

"You are welcome, niece Mary Ann."

And so they opened the door of the nice little parlor, and took the sick, homeless widow in.

Aunt Roxy had remained standing in precisely the same spot where she was when she took the baby. She was afraid to move, she had an indefinite fear, that if she did, she should crush some of the soft little bones that lay all smothered up in the blankets. It was worse than that roll of Honiton lace she had been so afraid of injuring, that she had two nervous headaches before Ellen Wood's bridal dress was fairly done. If it should move or cry now, she had a feeling that she should go into hysterics, and let it drop, of course.

Mrs. Starr, overcome at first by the excitement and fatigue of her arrival, did not notice either Aunt Roxy or the baby; but a little feeble cry, which went all over Aunt Roxy, like a shock from a galvanic battery, soon called her attention to it, and she held out her arms for the precious burthen.

Aunt Roxy laid it in them with a little tremor, as one feels when something very unusual has happened to them; but finding herself instantly relieved, repeated her sisters formal welcome, and met the pale upturned lips, which the niece offered to her, with a kiss.

The baby soon kicked his way out from the blankets, being now fairly awake, and having them all removed, showed to the curious aunts a little round bit of a human body without any hair on its head, a white chubby face, two large gray eyes, no nose to speak of, and a very wide mouth. There were arms, and two red fists, which it seemed to take special pleasure in doubling up, and throwing themselves about in all directions, as if they were in a great fury and anxious to fight somebody, though whom it was very doubtful, for they came oftener in contact with its own face than with any one's else. What a queer little thing it was! One would have thought, to have seen the wondering and timid glances which the old aunts cast toward it, as it lay stretching and fighting in its mother's lap, that it was a new species for the first time discovered and brought to light.

The stage did not "put up" in Mountford, it was only a way station, and the gentleman who had accompanied Mrs. Starr from the West, could not remain longer than to see her safely into her new home. The parting between them was brief, but affecting. He had been very kind to the sick widow, and she felt exceedingly grateful. He had become attached to her in her patient, uncomplaining suffering, and he knew that this parting was until they should meet where sickness and death never come.

The aunts heard the blessing, and understood the deep significance of his parting wish—"May Jesus, our divine and human friend, be near and comfort you."

Notwithstanding their anticipations of the change which this arrival would make in the family, the aunts found they had not begun to realize it.

Now, what to do first, with this weary, sick mother; and then, what with this staring, stretching baby. They stood still, looking at each other and at them, until Mrs. Starr, seeing or suspecting their dilemma, and being as yet not too feeble to assist herself, began to make preparations for "being at home." She put the baby on the floor, and laid aside her bonnet and shawl, looking far less sick than when she entered, and after having occupied herself a little while in this way, the power of thinking and moving seemed to come to the aunts, and they began to stir themselves in good earnest, to carry out some of the many hospitable plans they had made for the reception of their guests.

Aunt Cily hurried to get tea, while Aunt Roxy put away "the things," which the arrival had strewed about, and brought out from the sitting-room one of the little sewing chairs, which, strange to say, proved precisely the thing in which to tend baby.

It was very plain, from the moment the stage which brought Mrs. Starr rolled away, she had not come to be a burden. Sick or not, so long as she could move she intended to. She showed it, tired as she was, in the way she folded up the baby's blankets as she took them off. She showed it now, in the care with which she smoothed the small rug which had been pushed away by Aunt Roxy's nervous way of pulling in the sewing-chair.

If she had gone to work to make a most elaborate plea of weakness, and intention, notwithstanding, to help herself, it would have passed for nothing with the aunts, in comparison with these two little acts of careful consideration.

"She has lots of the Denton in her, and looks enough like her mother to be Cynthia herself, come back from her grave," whispered Roxy to

Cily, as they were both busy over the cooking-stove, preparing the tea.

"She is her very image," returned Cily, "and if she has got a consumption at all, it ain't galloping; I know enough about sickness to be sure of that."

They had planned the tea-tray, with the fine damask napkin, for a cover, for this first night's tea. It was to be carried in, and placed near the chrysanthemums, so "to be cheerful like." But while they were proceeding with these preparations, they heard a soft voice say, close to them, in the kitchen:

"Is there nothing I can do to help you; I am quite able. I feel better than I have for weeks. Oh what a cunning, beautiful kitchen; it looks like wax-work itself; I never saw any thing so perfect."

"It isn't so clean as it might be," said Aunt Cily, looking around with a disparaging face; "but Roxy and I, we do our own work, and sometimes we get so driven with our sewing that we haven't any time for any thing else."

"I don't see what you could find to do here, if you had no sewing. Don't you put your tea table out here? How nice it will be; do let me help you!"

The sisters looked at each other with much surprise. Had she heard all they had said about the trouble of moving the table into the sitting-room, and having it exposed so constantly to their frequent callers? Did she know, that among all the changes which they had feared, this was the very worst? But no, of course she did not; and it was "just like Cynthia, to think of every thing," so without a hint of any other intentions, they put out the same old table at which they had sat alone for years, but which was made for four.

While they were thus busy, and, in their shy way becoming a little acquainted, the hands of the two aunts were arrested in their occupation, as suddenly as if seized invisibly; for out over the house, clear, shrill, and it must be confessed, rather noisily, broke a cry, so new that the very panes of window-glass seemed to shake for a moment in astonishment. Up it swelled, clearer and louder every instant, and every instant their trepidation increased, until it became visible even to Mrs. Starr. "Oh," she said, "that is only the baby; he has had a nice long nap, and is telling his mother he is all ready for his tea too," and she went to bring him.

"His tea!" repeated Aunt Roxy; "you would not put another plate and knife and fork on the table, would you, Cily?"

"Why, yes, perhaps so, for manners' sake," answered Aunt Cily, hesitatingly; "but, of course he can't eat much."

"I wonder what he does eat;" and, as the baby screamed louder and louder, the nerves of the aunts evidently were giving way; "I guess I better just go and ask;" so Aunt Roxy crept to the parlor door, and, opening it a little crack, whispered in:

"Mary Ann, what now *can* that baby eat for his supper?"

"A little new milk, if you have it, thank you," said the young mother. "He is so hungry that he is eating his fists off; and, not finding them very good, he means to have us know it."

The door shut quickly, but very softly; and, running into the kitchen with a celerity she had not shown for years, Roxy seized a small tin pail and her sun-bonnet, and only stopping to say "He is eating up his fists, poor baby," she disappeared.

Aunt Cily sat down very helplessly in a chair by the table, the news that the baby "was eating his fists" had "capped the climax;" there was nothing left to come next.

In a very short time Aunt Roxy made her appearance, with the bright tin pail running over with rich new milk; and as the baby's hurry prevented his mother from rendering any very efficient assistance, she took her first lesson in preparing the much talked of "nus bottle."

And now, who ever saw such an operation as this of feeding? Why, how he choked and strangled, and pulled the bottle to his mouth, and pushed it away again, and kicked and cried, and let the milk run down upon the sides of his face, and his clean feeding-cloth, and how coolly niece Mary Ann took it all; putting away the angry fists, and holding the bottle tight to his mouth, strangle or no strangle, until he began to drink, and then, how she called him "a very naughty little boy, indeed," in a voice which sounded very much as if she was saying just the opposite; and shook him, but so lovingly, that the baby turned his gray eyes up to her, and stopped drinking, just long enough to smile.

All this was a mystery to Aunt Roxy, not that she had never seen a baby fed before; indeed she had, many hundreds of them; but it was a very different thing, this baby that was one day to be *theirs*. She appropriated it with that wonderful mother's instinct, which was there, though it had never wakened before, and which, in coming now, in answer to the child's call, shook the old maiden aunt's frame with an emotion unaccountable, and beyond her control. The same thing made her take the child as it drained the last drop from the bottle, and, putting her long, bony arms about it, walk up and down the room, while her lips, for the first time, uttered the expressive baby lullaby—"Sish! sish! sish!"

"He is so good with you," said Mrs. Starr, regarding the two with much admiration, "that I will go and help Aunt Cily. I want him to learn to know and love you;" and for the first time since she came there was a tremor in her voice; still she smiled cheerfully, and went out.

What a tea it was! The invalid, with that keen appetite, which is a symptom of her disease, thought she had never sat down to such a table before; and the aunts, with a pride and pleasure, which they took no pains to conceal, saw the enjoyment and the rest which came to their guest as she partook of their liberally-supplied dainties.

After tea, with a bashfulness which was very ludicrous, the cradle was produced and admired, as it deserved to be, and the plump baby was duly installed in it. An old easy-chair, which had been stowed in a corner of their own bed-room, and never shown, though it was neatly covered with pretty old-fashioned linen patch, was brought out and placed in the cosiest corner, by the cheerful fire place. That night, before the lamp was lighted, the bright blaze shone out not only over the good dead men upon the walls, and upon the straight, thin figures of the maiden sisters, but on the wicker cradle and the sleeping babe, and the pale young mother, who sat with a beating, grateful heart, thanking God that in all her afflictions He had "remembered mercy," and that her lines had fallen to her in such "pleasant places." And when, at the appointed hour, Aunt Cily brought the great family Bible, that had her own and Mary's mother's name, written together on the leaf that contained the family record, and having read in a clear, cultivated voice, with the dear old-time accents, a portion from its pages, knelt down to offer no common prayer, in no common language,—then, more than ever, the two words, "pleasant places," came soothingly over the widow's heart, and went with her to a long refreshing sleep.

III.

The Legacy.

THE next day Mountford was in quite a state of excitement, over the arrival at the house of the maiden sisters. They had mentioned their expectation of it to no one but their minister, Rev. Mr. White; but the stage was seen to stop, and a woman and her baby to have been deposited, so it came very soon to be known, not only that they had certainly come, but also many little details of their history, some of which were, and many were not, true. Sufficient, however, was known to excite the curiosity of the villagers, and they received so many calls that, long before the day was half over, Mrs. Starr began to show symptoms of fatigue, which immediately recalled to the aunts her condition, and made them insist upon banishing her to the parlor, while they kept the cradle and the baby to gratify kind inquirers.

"You're just as handy at it," said old Mrs. Ware, who had come to inquire about the cradle, "as if you had brought up as large a family as I have. See there now, Aunt Roxy turns the feet and not the head, when she wants to turn the baby, and that is more than half your own mothers think of, a muddling and a riling up the brains as if they wa'n't of no account, no way. It beats every thing, to see how handy you are; but what is the baby's name?"

"Isaac Starr," said Aunt Cily, with a dignified look, as if she was conferring a blessing.

"Are you sure?" asked Roxy.

"Well, no, now; I can't say I am. I don't think his mother has called him anything but 'baby, or blossom, or my rose-bud, or pink, or pet, or darling,' or some such name, since she came."

"No more she 'aint," said Aunt Roxy, thoughtfully; "I will just step in and ask her what it really is—may be it *is* Isaac."

She returned in a moment, with a most wo-begone expression of face; "His name," she said, "is Anthony Starr, named after his father; but his mother calls him, and she says she should like to have us, 'Tony—Tony, who ever heard of such a name—Tony Starr!"

Aunt Cily's face conveyed even more dismay than her tone, and she said briefly, "We will have it altered to Isaac."

"I think not," said Aunt Roxy; "she seemed to like it just as it is. It is strange what notions some folks take about names—Tony Starr! Tony Starr! I never knew anything beat it."

The baby, with a dim, indistinct idea, that he was hearing something which sounded familiarly, held up his head and looked round on the listeners, almost as if he meant to say, "It's a right, good name, and I should just like to see who dares question it."

Mrs. Ware said, "he looked very bright and active for such a child, and she dared say, if it hadn't inherited nothing from its mother, it might live to make a man, though its name was Tony; for her part, she rather fancied it. She was sure it was better than an old Jew's name, if he was the father of the faithful. She had had eight boys, and not one of them had to bear a Scripture name, for Mr. Ware always said she had so much bother with them, it was only fair she should choose her own names. Tony! Tony Starr—very good, indeed." So she kissed little Tony on both his fat, red cheeks; but he blubbered, as if he did not take it for much of a compliment, and had not the least intention in the world of returning it. One visitor to-day was very acceptable, that was Mr. White. He was an excellent minister; such an one as with any other denomination would hardly have found his way to the small village. He was cultivated, had seen much of the world, and, above all, possessed that first excellence for his profession—sincere and devoted piety. Unassuming and quiet, he yet carried so much warm, earnest zeal into his work, that he was every where, not only the beloved, but the eminently successful minister of Christ. Particularly was he precious to those who were in affliction; having seen much sorrow himself, he could feel for, and sympathize with them, and this he did, not in any ostentatious, common-place way, but often only by the pressure of a hand, the dropping of a tear, the whispered prayer, the invoked blessing, or, it may be, by merely the quotation of an appropriate passage of Scripture, or one of those lines of sacred hymns which always speak so closely to the heart bereaved.

If Mrs. Starr had seen occasion to thank God so sincerely on the previous night, for the "pleasant places," to-night, after a short but delightful interview with her new minister, she found much greater need. Indeed, she regarded it, and justly, as the choicest boon that could now have been given her—this gentle, sympathizing friend, and this devoted, holy teacher. With what nice tact and delicacy, even in that first short interview, had he drawn from her those feelings she had thought would never again be uttered by her to any earthly friend ; how tenderly he had spoken of her loss. How the tears ran down his cheeks when he told her of his young bride, that he had laid asleep many years ago, in a distant graveyard, and how fresh and bright his hopes were of seeing her again, when his Master, having no more for him to do here, should call him to be for ever united to her.

When he left her, Aunt Roxy found her with small red spots on both cheeks. She knew very well what they were ; but Mr. White had said a word, as he passed through the sitting-room, about cheerfulness being the very best medicine they could give their niece ; so Aunt Roxy looked round, as if she wanted to wheel up the sofa they had never owned near the fire for the invalid, but not finding it, she contented herself with tipping the old easy chair back, and placing sticks of wood under the legs, a very good substitute, indeed, but not perfectly satisfactory to her; for, in a whispered consultation, which she held with Aunt Cily soon after leaving the room, it was decided that the very next day, Aunt Cily should go to a town near and buy a new sofa. Then the old aunts brought the small hair-covered trunk, which they kept under their bed, and which contained all the money they were able to lay up,—they asking no interest, but security,—and from it they counted out, in shining half dollars, the necessary sum; and, with that cheerful giving, which their God saw and loved, the good old maidens never hesitated—never said to themselves, grudgingly, we haye earned it by the hardest work, and have lived without a sofa all our lives, it seems grievous that we must spend it now for only a sister's child. Oh, no, they had no such thoughts; they gave it cheerfully, and as they did, they said softly to themselves, "feed my lambs!"

Not a word was said to Mrs. Starr about the new purchase, and the first she knew of it—it was brought into her room.

A very nice, rich couch it was, just the thing for her failing strength. And when once laid upon it, she had such an expression of intense rest, that the aunts looked at her and admired both her and it, with very much the same astonished admiration with which they had regarded the baby in his straw-basket cradle. Both were a very unexpected addition to the dress-makers' house; but for both there was, as we have seen, readily found a place.

These changes were, however, only visible and outward signs of the great changes which had taken place, not only within the family, but in the whole town of Mountford. No one had realized, or would have believed it, had they been told what important personages Miss Cily and Miss Roxy were in every domestic establishment. For the first two weeks after Mrs. Starr's arrival, they obstinately refused all work. Mrs. Dean could not go to New York without that new silk dress; "and Mr. Dean could not let his business stand still just because there were some new comers." But this somewhat caustic appeal fell on deafened ears. Miss Cily would "run in one hour and fit the lining, if that would be any accommodation," but she neither would nor could set a stitch. Jane Remson had torn every school-dress off her back, and must stay at home if that ninepenny calico couldn't be made up. "If Jane would run in about nine, after Mary Ann and the baby were both asleep, they would try to get it out, so some seamstress could finish it, but for the present their work was done. It was perfectly astonishing, both to them and every one else, now they could not be had, in what demand they were. Every one's wardrobe seemed to be thrown in a state of most inextricable confusion. And Mrs. Dean threatened, very loudly, "to import a girl who would stick to her business, when she returned from New York."

At first, to use Aunt Cily's words, "all this discomflutterated them very much." They were naturally obliging, and as their life's experience had shown, were quite willing to work for their customers, often at very great inconvenience to themselves; but now, they really had neither time nor nerves for the calls upon them, and as one of the two things must be given up, they were not long in deciding which. Indeed, though Mrs. Deacon Dexter told them it was "a gospel duty to clothe the naked," they held it very light in comparison with the one of feeding the Lamb which had taken such possession of their heads and hearts.

For the first two weeks after her arrival, Mrs. Starr had many days when she was able to be around with them, and initiate them into the mysteries of baby tending. Never once did she say "she feared she and her boy would be a great trouble to them." Never did she hint at any of the doubts, and dreads, and fears which seemed at times almost to shut out heaven from her sight; but she very quietly and sensibly talked over with them the future, expressed many wishes with regard to little Tony, and told the aunts many traits of his dead father, which she felt sure would reappear in his child, and would require a line of treatment, which she judiciously marked out. While she never spoke of her own death as if an event likely to take place very soon, she seemed to be deliberately and carefully planning for her absence. She did not even annoy them by too frequent and warm expressions of her gratitude for the daily exertions and sacrifices which she saw they were making for her, but she showed how grateful and appreciative she was by many words and deeds which they could not but understand. She warmly urged, after the first few days, their resuming their usual occupation, and even offered to assist them. As for little Tony, she said it was better for him to begin life by learning to take care of himself. So he stretched, and kicked, and grew, lying on the floor, or in his little cradle, hour after hour, perfectly contented with this kind of existence, as he knew no other.

By degrees, in this way, seeing he was, as Aunt

Roxy said, "neither sugar nor salt," they began to regard him as coming a little more within the line of human and possible things. They could take him up or turn him over if he began to give unmistakable evidence of being too weary of his position, could even begin to administer the "nus bottle," and as for "trotting," Aunt Cily was a proficient in it from the very beginning. The first time her heels struck the floor after the light burden was placed in her lap, they fell to a natural kind of tune, which was only by degrees exchanged for beating time to some sweet, low, Methodist hymn, sung often, very often, at the pleasant social meetings, but never to such a kind of listener as this before. Little Tony, however, seemed to have a wonderful power of appreciation, for several times, when every other effort had failed of getting him to sleep, she had taken him, and and watched, with most intense satisfaction the process by which, after all manner of contortions and fightings, he at last yielded to the power of the music. Sometimes, Aunt Cily would find she had soothed both children at the same time; and would look up to convey, by some curious movement, the report of the victory, to find the mother's eyes too, closed, and her pale young face drooping on the pillow.

Thus the first month passed. Every thing settled down so naturally and so pleasantly at the cottage, that really it seemed almost impossible to the aunts to remember that there ever had been any other life. They began to resume their work, but with much care not to overtask themselves, and always with the proviso, that if either "Mary Ann or the baby needed them, they might give up what they had commenced, at a moment's warning." Mrs. Starr, by a plea of needing the amusement which the occupation would afford her, found an opportunity to render them a little help; but, indeed, it was but little she could do, for her hands grew weaker and weaker every day, and it was very easy to see, that what she had accomplished one week, was far beyond her power the next. It was astonishing how much ingenuity the maiden aunts showed in procuring for her diversion. One morning, if she had past a comfortable night, and felt able to talk, they would bring in good Mr. White to comfort her, and when he staid as long as he thought best, they would continue the book he had been reading; or, in their quaint, hearty way, follow out, much to her enjoyment, a train of thought which he had started. And then, at other times, when they saw her eye grow dim, and they knew by that instinct which is a free masonry between kind hearts, that her thoughts were dwelling painfully on the loved and lost, they would exhaust all the store-house of treasures they had been accumulating for years. Their very piece bags were made to minister to her cheerfulness. Many a long story of weal or woe, being connected with the making up of this dress, of which the bit of calico was a sample; or with that silk, which was destined for a peculiar person or occasion. Often Mrs. Starr made from the choicest of these bits some small cushion or curiously shaped needle-book, all of which trinkets her aunts regarded with a peculiar admiration and veneration, and laid carefully away.

One day, Mrs. Starr found among these treasures, a piece of thick white satin, about a quarter of a yard square. This she begged of Aunt Roxy, and taking some delicate blue working silk, she spent many hours of every day working upon it. Whatever it was, she did not seem disposed to show it, or make it an object of remark, though she took no particular pains to conceal it.

It was very obvious, however, that it was a matter of much interest to her, and that for some reason, it had many sad associations. The aunts often found her in tears, with it in her hand, and never knew her to put it aside without betraying many symptoms of extreme fatigue. Indeed, they began to regard the small piece of satin with a real dread before her task was finished. It was then folded carefully and placed in a blue velvet bag, which was also tastefully and delicately embroidered. This was put in a paper covering, and an address written upon it. Then the whole was placed in the Bible, which became every day Mrs. Starr's almost inseparable companion. When this was done, a sense of relief seemed to come to the widow, and there followed one of those temporary changes for the better, which so often give hope in her disease.

She came every day to the pleasant sitting-room, played often and fondly with the baby, and, so it seemed to her anxious nurses, was really beginning to take a new hold on life.

They were making plans for rather enlarging their business in the coming spring, in order to meet the increasing expenditures of their family, when, all at once, the new life was lost. Mrs. Starr grew so visibly and rapidly feeble, that not even Mr. White, who had always been the most sanguine and hopeful, spoke of her continuing with them but a short time longer.

Old Dr. Townsend, who had been in attendance since she came, said the "breaking up of winter would break her up too, and it would be almost a wonder, if she lived to see the first spring flower."

Now, although this had been the event which the aunts had anticipated before her arrival, and which they had certainly not forgotten since, it almost seemed to them, (so different is the reality of death from any thing of which we can conceive,) as if they heard it for the first time. They were both awed and shocked by its near approach, and seemed to themselves standing on a strange, mysterious ground, with a life begun and a life ending, encircling them. At times they became really confused and incapable of any of the exertions which were required from them, and at such times nothing seemed to have the effect of restoring them to self-control, but the calm advice and prayers of their minister.

It was easier for Mr. White to soothe and comfort the dying one, than to bring clearly before these bewildered minds just what God meant for them to do.

"If she only might live," Cily would say, "until this boy got through his first teeth, it would not be half so hard to have her go; but the poor little fellow what will become of him now. It is a very inscrutable providence."

"Oh, Miss Cily," Mr. White would answer, "God can take care of the baby's first teeth as well as He can of the old man's last. You must learn to have more confidence in Him."

"But all the sins, and naughty things, he will be doing when he grows up," Miss Roxy would continue, "and no parents to counsel and direct him."

"When his father and mother forsake him," Miss Roxy, we must not forget who has promised to 'take him up.' Have trust in Him. He has never called on you for it before to any great extent; are you going to deny it to Him now?"

"You must both learn this lesson from this young mother. Do you suppose she is dying without any throbs of anxiety for the future of this child? and yet have you heard a word from her which has shown that she is afraid to leave him with God? It seems to me every time I leave Mrs. Starr's bedside, as if I had been conversing with an angel; she is already half in heaven, and you would not call her back, by showing any of this distrust, this want of faith, yourselves."

Thus fortified, the aunts were enabled to conceal from the dying mother to a great extent the fears and solicitude which had already, even within these few weeks, added so many more gray hairs to their heads.

Cheerfully and patiently, a wonder to themselves and every one else, they tended and cared for the dying; and when before the earliest flowers came, as the doctor had prophesied, they closed her eyes and folded her emaciated hands over her still breast; they knew that a mother was lost on earth, but a new ministering angel had entered heaven; they knew that upon another orphan had fallen the greatest of earthly losses; but that that loss was also his gain, as it had made him the inheritor of God's most sacred promises. And they turned from the dead to the living, with an earnest prayer that they might be enabled so to perform their duty to the orphan, that when they should again meet his mother, it might be with the words upon their lips, "Have we not 'fed your lamb?'"

Mrs. Starr had nothing to leave her son but a few small keepsakes, her Bible, and some choice letters, which she had received from his father. Of all of these, she had spoken to her aunts, and had designated the year of his life, in which she wished them presented to him. When they returned from her grave, and went to the desolated parlor, they saw the Bible just where she had last placed it, on the table, by the side of the new sofa. As Aunt Roxy took it to put it carefully away, a small flat paper neatly sewed up fell out. She recognized it at once, as the one which enclosed the bit of white satin upon which Mrs. Starr had been so long busily working. Picking it up, Aunt Roxy read on the outside, written in a very distinct hand, these words:

"Tony Starr's Legacy; to be given to him when he reaches his tenth year."

"Tony Starr's Legacy!" repeated Aunt Roxy, turning the little bundle curiously over and over. "What can it be? I thought they had not one cent in the world, and yet here it is, just in the shape of a small will. Perhaps now, after all, the father did own a mint of money in western lands, which by the time he is ten years old, will be worth, no one knows how much. Cily, sister Cily! do come here a moment!"

Aunt Cily, who was busy trotting Tony in the sitting-room, came immediately in, and seeing the paper, recognized it, as Roxy had, but was not quite so ready to adopt the theory of the western lands. "Put it away very carefully," she said, "may be it will prove something which will be worth more than silver and gold to him. His mother seemed to have a kind of instinct as to what was best for the child. See here, Roxy, he is kicking and crowing for it now, as if he had an idea that it was meant for his good."

And so Tony was; struggling and pushing forward toward either it, or Aunt Roxy, it would have been difficult to tell which; for Aunt Roxy had of late taken most of the care of him, while her sister devoted herself to the sick mother; therefore, the baby already seemed to set up a superior claim upon her, which, of course, Aunt Roxy never for a moment knew how to resist.

Just now, however, she was too much occupied with this small peculiar paper parcel, to take any notice of him. She turned it over and over in her hands. She held it up to the window and let the bright light strike directly through it, but it told no tales. She weighed it carefully in her hands. It was much to heavy for any thing beside the real parchment, on which a will would be written.

If she could but loosen the threads which were so neatly stitched to hold it together, she could easily put them in again, and it would be such a satisfaction to see it written in good black and white letters, in his father's own hand-writing, the conveyance made when he found his death was inevitable, of land, western land, rising every day of this boy's life in value, until, when he began to need it, and they could do little for him, he should turn out to be quite an heir.

Now, Aunt Cily very well knew, that with all her excellent traits sister Roxy had a natural share of woman's curiosity, much more than she had, and she was accustomed to dealing with it rather sharply, so she said now :

"Don't be fooling with that, Roxy, the first thing you know you'll want to be opening it; and it's sealed with something stronger than if Mary Ann had put it in an iron safe, locked it up, and thrown the key to the bottom of the ocean, to stay there until Tony's tenth birth-day."

"What!" said Aunt Roxy, evidently very much puzzled.

"What?" and Aunt Cily's voice had an additional tinge of sharpness. "Honor!" Put it back in the Bible, and put the Bible away. Don't you feel as if those great, large eyes were looking at you this very moment to see that you are doing your duty?"

Aunt Roxy gave a little start, and looked over her shoulder toward the deserted "prophet's-room," but instantly replaced the paper in the Bible, folded the Bible in a fine linen pocket-handkerchief which had belonged to Mrs. Starr, tied around it very tightly a neat white cord, then sewed it up with some fine stitches, and at last, deposited it with the other treasures in the third bureau drawer.

All this had cost Aunt Roxy at first a considerable effort; she did wish to know what the legacy was; and nine years from now, when it was to be opened, neither Cily nor she might be there to read it. But it had only needed the reproof which she received, to make her see her error. And so, until his tenth year, was laid away Tony Starr's Legacy.

IV.

Tony's First Punishment.

AFTER the conversation they had with which Mr. White regarding the exercise of more confidence in God in their care of Tony, it had seemed to the good aunts to be just precisely such a matter in which they must rely upon prayers, and the silent but constant answers to them. They had also now,—and in bringing this out, I would beg leave to call the attention of my readers to one of the most important objects of my book,—they had now a great source of help in the reliance, which they felt, not only upon their own prayers, but upon the answer to the prayers which the dead parents and grandparents of the child had offered, it may be long years ago. Mr. White had been at much pains to impress upon them the number and variety of promises by which

God had expressly declared his intention to have the children benefited by the holy lives and prayers of their ancestors; that at times they had rather a clouded mingling of Hannah, saying, "For this child I prayed, and the Lord has given me the petition which I asked of him, and the prayers of their young, dying niece Mary Ann." Every verse contained in the Abrahamic covenant became to them "more precious than apples of gold."

"I will establish my covenant between me and thee, and thy seed after thee, in their generations, for an everlasting covenant, to be a God unto thee and to thy seed after thee."

"Choose life, that both thou and thy seed may live."

"The Lord was gracious unto them, and had compassion on them, and had respect unto them, because of his covenant with Abraham, Isaac, and Jacob, and would not destroy them, neither cast he them from his presence as yet."

"The mercy of the Lord is from everlasting to

everlasting upon them that fear him, and his righteousness unto children's children; To such as keep his covenant, and to those that remember his commandments to do them."

"As for me, this is my covenant with them, saith the Lord; my spirit that is upon thee, and my words which I have put in thy mouth, shall not depart out of thy mouth, nor out of the mouth of thy seed, nor out of the mouth of thy seed's seed, saith the Lord, from henceforth and for ever."

"The promise is unto you, and to your children."

"Jesus Christ was a minister of the circumcision for the truth of God, to confirm the promises made unto the fathers."

"If ye be Christ's then are ye Abraham's seed, and heirs according to the promise."

These verses the aunts had read many, many times during their long religious life, but how different they seemed to them now. And this is one of the strongest proofs that the Bible is in truth God's word. In our hours of trouble we find new life, hope, comfort, springing up from what had always been before to us simply sacred as words of holy writ. A new sorrow, a new joy; and to our surprise, thousands of years ago, some other human heart had passed through the same; and He who made so, who knoweth our down sitting and uprisings, and who is acquainted with all our ways, had spoken words of comfort to meet this very emergency.

So it was with the old Abrahamic covenant, given long ago to that wandering Jewish tribe, and coming now with the freshness and strength of eternal truth to support and cheer these two old maiden aunts in the education and daily and hourly life of a little orphan boy. Surely never were truer words than these, which we find coming from the inspired pen of Paul in his epistle to the Romans.

"Whatsoever things were written aforetime, were written for our learning that we, through patience and comfort of the scriptures, might have hope."

"Possibly their own prayers, all filled with sins and pollution," so thought these godly women, might fail to come up before the mercy-seat, but those of Cynthia and her holy husband, and Mary Ann, "already," as Mr. White had said, while here, "an angel, and half in heaven," must have been accepted, registered, and sealed with the great covenant seal.

Now it may be supposed, that while these thoughts were very satisfactory, and in truth of much practical value to the aunts, they did not assist them in taking the personal care of Tony. The very first night after her death, —for, until her last hour, Mrs. Starr had been able, and did speak often and tenderly to her child,—so on this first night, when her voice was stilled for ever, a sense of his loss seemed to have been almost made known to the crying and terrified babe. He screamed for hours, only stopping long enough to listen now and then for the answering voice that never before was mute to his call; and then, when too exhausted to cry any longer, he moaned and moaned, until the poor aunts, weak and wearied beyond the power of any effectual exertion, by all the crowding events of the day and night, were obliged to call in a young mother from the neighbourhood, who, after many of the little arts which she knew so well, at last succeeded in quieting and putting him to sleep.

But it was a night which, to the last day of their lives, the aunts never forgot, and of which, for the first week, they saw a frequent recurrence, though never so severe or long protracted. At the end of the second month after his mother's death, Tony seemed to become more reconciled to the event, or at least, to have come to the conclusion that no effort on his part would bring her back; so he began gradually to learn the little baby ways which he had at first stoutly resisted. He consented to sit alone, even caught with much eagerness at the pretty tin rattle which Aunt Roxy had walked a mile to buy; and from being a crying, fretful child, suddenly subsided into a happy, merry, noisy boy. Oh what a joyful day this was at the cottage. It was impossible to praise and admire him enough. One of the aunts was constantly saying, "Dear little Tony! good boy! good boy!" or "Precious little Lamb, he may be as happy as a king if he wants to, so he may! his auntie says he may."

As may be supposed, this incessant, anxious care of the child, told most sensibly upon the sisters. Every body in Mountford had thought them so thin before the baby came that they could not be thinner; but now, to their astonishment, they realized that they could change; and, "dear me, how old they grow—it makes me feel really sorry to see them. I am afraid they will go in a consumption, too. No wonder, a great boy like that to come right into a woman's arms without her being used to it before; why it is enough to wear any body out, soul and body too." Such were some of the remarks which their appearance excited every time they left their own house.

Dressmaking was not at present to be thought

of; so they saw, with very different feelings from what they ever had before, a new sign put up next to the Post-office—"Misses M. & G. Gillett, Dressmakers and Milliners."

They had no time or thought for any thing or any body but Tony, and their own souls; of course to neglect these, would be not only to injure themselves, but most seriously and certainly to injure him; so they faithfully and tenaciously adhered to all their religious privileges, only now, for the first time, they were separated in their enjoyment of them, for one must always "stay at home with the baby."

Certainly, amidst all this, the maiden aunts were very uncomplaining; though they knew, full well, how much of quiet comfort and happiness they had lost since the little guest came.

The warm summer weather had now come, and in it, Tony's growth and development was a wonder even to the most experienced mothers, but a constant source of the greatest astonishment and admiration to his aunts.

As we have before said, they were fond of the birds, the bees, and their flowers, and when they found how dearly Tony loved to get down on the soft, green grass, and lie with his eyes watching the dancing leaves, or the nodding flowers, they always brought him out, whenever the day would allow, and spent many of the hours when during other summers they had been closely confined to their work playing with, or watching him in reality, while to themselves and to others they seemed to be busy about their garden or their yard.

Summer was not through before Tony, despising the ignoble rest of the soft, sheltered spot, began to creep round after them, and then began a new world of anxiety; why, they had just become accustomed to his helplessness, when they began to be troubled by his helpfullness, and to find to their sorrow, that with the power of locomotion, he had just in proportion the power of getting into mischief.

He would creep to the spot where Aunt Roxy

had planted the choicest verbena seed, and before she could get to him, with the power of imitation, which, in truth, he did develop rather remarkably, would put his little hands into the nicely covered, exactly planted row, and would scatter them literally to "the four winds of heaven;" or, attracted with bright tulips, he would make a rapid onslaught from the nook into which Aunt Cily had tucked him, rattle and all, and before her slow, old steps could reach him, notwithstanding her sharp, quick calls, would pick the yellow, red, pink, and white, toss them up, screaming and shouting with delight as the many-colored shower fell thick upon him.

And then, it was very ludicrous to witness the half amused and half terrified looks with which his aunts regarded him. Why, he was worse than the chickens; more destructive than Ned Palmer's white rabbits, when they broke into the garden. "Was there ever in this world such a child?" This was the exclamation they made many times every day; the only difference being in the expression with which their faces and voices conveyed it. Sometimes it was one of the most undisguised admiration; sometimes one of wonder and inquiry; but oftenest, it must be owned, one of perplexity, in other words, simply, "What shall we do with this boy?"

And now it was rather singular to see what a variety and quantity of advice they received. No one supposed *they* knew any thing about babies; how could they? So there was enough mental and bodily medicine prescribed to have killed a whole township of children, but fortunately Tony was too healthy to require the one, and too great a pet to get many doses of the other. People would insist on marvelling that the child lived, but in spite of it all, he did live, and "grew exceedingly," and it almost seemed that in proportion as he prospered, his good old aunts withered and pined away. This would never do; the child would lose his home, and be doubly an orphan, if some relief could not be obtained; so Mr. White once more came in with some sensible advice, which he had borrowed from his wife, and picked up in his years of close observation. First, he insisted upon a little more efficient discipline. What if Tony did prefer to be walked to sleep every night in the arms of one of his aunts, instead of being put into his cradle, that was no reason why he should be allowed to do it. He was too old; it was only injuring him; and then, if he preferred to have one of the best tumblers, and a teaspoon to rattle against it, instead of his proper rattle, it was only the more reason why it should be taken firmly away, and he punished if he persisted in crying for it.

It would be very useless to enter into the details of discipline which Mr. White, with the freedom and plainness of a favorite minister, felt at liberty to make. The only trouble in the whole was, that though intending to follow his advice, and considering it as they did, very wise and good, Tony's aunts, neither of them, so far, had the courage to do so.

The summer was fairly over, and the chill of the early fall mornings made it impossible to allow Tony the much enjoyed pleasure of creeping around in the clean, green sward of the little yard. But what did he know or care for early fall, or colds in the head, or on the lungs? He only knew of the blue sky, and the pretty, bright sunshine, and the moving, noisy, beautiful world that lay without that small, white door. So one morning, when it was unusually bleak and raw, he put on his hood (he had not yet arrived at the manhood of a cap), and creeping up to the door, laid himself down flat on his back and began to kick his heels very noisily against it, while he uttered the peculiar sound with which he was accustomed to solicit the favor.

"Hear him, Cily!" said Roxy, with a face of much distress; "he wants to go out of doors, dear little fellow, what shall we do."

"Why," said Aunt Cily, "it's as raw and cold as November; of course he can't go. Tony! good little Tony, here is a pretty ball, come and see Aunt Cily roll it for him. There it goes, way—way—way—off. Now, Tony, run and pick it up, and we'll try again."

Tony followed the ball a moment with his grey eyes, but showed no intention to "pick it up," or to stop more than a minute from the kicking on the door, and the begging cry.

"Dear little Tony!" said Aunt Cily, changing her tactics. "Here is Aunt Cily dancing up and down, up and down, in the great big looking-glass, Tony, come and dance too."

This was an operation of which Tony was remarkably fond. He had danced his aunt's arms until they seemed as if they would drop off, many times before, but to-day it had lost its charm, he would not move; kick! kick! beg! beg! without an instant's intermission. The aunts exchanged many anxious and inquiring glances, but neither ventured an opinion until the noise could not be borne any longer; then Aunt Roxy said,

"Cily, I think, as Mr. White told us, it is ruining the boy to allow him to take on so. We ought either to let him go out, or to make him get up and stop."

Aunt Cily went to the window, and looked out very longingly. There were the dry leaves sweeping in little eddies all up and down the yard, the angry grey clouds and the murky air almost heavy now with coming snow.

"He can't go," she said, with a despairing shake of the head; "he would catch his death of cold."

"Then make him get up and be quiet here; I declare, my head spins round like a top."

"Get up, Tony!" said Aunt Cily, standing at a distance, and speaking very gruffly.

Tony began to knock his head as well as heels, by way of reply, but did not move.

"Get up this instant, you naughty boy;" and Aunt Cily stepped a little nearer.

Tony looked wonderingly up in her face for a minute, and then pitched his voice a note or two louder, by way of reply.

"Get right up," interposed Aunt Roxy, looking on through her spectacles from a corresponding distance on the other side of him; "don't you hear your Aunt Cily speak? Dear little Tony must be a good boy, and mind at once when his aunts speak to him. Mr. White says he must."

Now, Mr. White's authority was evidently no more to Tony than Aunt Cily's, so he only turned his face, very red with his continued screaming, toward the door.

"Get up this minute," said Aunt Roxy, whose temper began to be a little nettled by this cool persistency, "or—or—I shall *punish you.*"

These last two words dropped from Aunt Roxy's mouth like a bullet, suddenly and with a great deal of force; but had she touched off a cannon, it would hardly have frightened her more. She looked as if she had done a dreadful thing, nor was she in the least relieved by Aunt Cily's immediate remark.

"There now, Roxy, you are in for it; don't you know Mr. White said, and his mother too, that we must not threaten to punish him, without doing so if he persisted? I am very sorry you did; I dare say I might have coaxed him in a few minutes. I was going for a tin pail and spoon."

"What shall I do?" asked Aunt Roxy, very helplessly.

"Now, there is but one thing you can do; make him get up, or punish him."

"How? how?"

"I don't know. I rather think you must box his ears."

"That may hurt his head."

"So it may. Solomon says, Spare the rod and spoil the child."

"A rod! why, that will hurt him too; what shall we do? Tony, dear little Tony, don't make such a dreadful noise; you make poor old Aunt Roxy's head ache very hard. Poor Aunt Roxy, cry." And the distressed aunt put her old, withered hands over her face, and began to cry so loud that Aunt Cily thought the noise she made even worse than Tony's.

Tony, who evidently thought this was a new species of play, crept upon his knees to Aunt Roxy, and began with much glee to pull her hands away from her face. Aunt Roxy let him pull at them for some time, only peeping at him now and then from between her fingers, while she made more doleful outcries than before. Tony began to laugh, and not only stood upon his feet, but allowed himself, holding tight on to the source of so much fun, to be drawn a little ways from the tempting door.

Aunt Roxy evidently considered herself triumphant, and was stealing a congratulatory glance at Cily, when Tony, taking advantage of the pause in the music, crept back to the door as fast as he could, and commenced precisely the same feats. Aunt Roxy's dismay was unbounded. Her throat was sore from the unusual exertion it made in the crying line, her nerves were tired, and she, to use her own expression, "pretty generally beat out." Could she begin and go all over the same process again. It was only better than the promised punishment, so with much reluctance, and so much less real ardor that it was totally inefficient, Aunt Roxy began again. She might have spared herself the trouble this time, for never was any thing more entirely thrown away. Tony not only would not listen, but struck violently at her as she put her face close to him to tempt him. There was no disguising the fact now; Tony was a very naughty boy.

Aunt Roxy took him firmly by both arms, and, with a hearty shake, put him on his feet, saying as she did so,

"Naughty, naughty Tony, stop; stop this minute."

Louder screams than ever. Tony evidently was not pleased with being shaken, but Aunt Roxy repeated the experiment with more decision, and the result was the same.

"That is only trifling with him, Roxy; you *must* make him mind now, or he is ruined for ever," said Aunt Cily, decidedly.

Aunt Roxy turned the fat little hand over until its palm lay in one of hers, and lifting her other, was about giving him summary punishment, when she suddenly stopped, and lifting the small rosy fingers to her mouth, kissed them over and over again.

"I can't," she said, "I can't, any how, Cily; just see what a darling he is."

"I see nothing but a very naughty boy, Roxy; and if you give him up now, never expect him to obey you again as long as you live, for he never will, that is certain."

Again Aunt Roxy's hand was lifted, and this time it came down on the lovingly held little fingers, but as gently as if it was only the oft-repeated love pat.

"There, there," said Aunt Roxy, repeating the pats when she saw the first had no very decidedly deadly effect. "There, now; will you stop crying and be a good boy?"

Tony, who was in truth easily amused, if he had a mind to be, looked up in her face, and a whole bevy of smiles chased away the tears.

"Pat-a-cake—pat-a-cake!" he said, in his most winning way; and in a moment Aunt Roxy and he were in a delightful frolic. "Pat-a-cake, baker, a man, and all," while Aunt Cily, standing by, looked on with quite as much pleasure.

"Mr. White was certainly right; all Tony required was a little firmness, and he would be the best boy in Mountford. How well it was Roxy had not given up to him in this first great battle," so quietly remarked Aunt Cily to herself.

V.

Tony's Progress.

AS winter was again approaching, and Tony began to run around the house, being no longer that most demanding of all things, a baby in arms, the aunts thought anxiously of the expenditures of the coming expensive season. They had earned so little during the past year that they were obliged to make frequent calls upon the small store which they had so laboriously accumulated for a "rainy day." It was very evident that Tony must be turned off a little more, and they resume their trade. In proposing to do so, they reaped the reward of their long years of fidelity. No seam ever ripped that they sewed, no hooks or eyes came off, until it was time they should; no whalebone ever intruded its black face where it was not desired. In short, their doing for others in the sewing line, just as they would that others should do for them, gave them now no distrust in their ability to regain the custom which had been transferred from them, to the new, fashionable dress-makers, with their patterns "direct from Paris by every steamer," as their advertisement in the "Mountford Gazette" very largely set off. As soon as it began to be whispered round, that Aunt Cily and Aunt Roxy were ready for work, it was astonishing how much there was to be done. How many of the new dresses, which had been cut by the Paris pattern, wanted "just taking up on the shoulder, or letting out under the arm;" how many had wrinkles that made the wearers "look like frights;" and how many brought new pieces, and new linings, to have the whole "done over right." The truth was, all Mountford had become so accustomed to the prim, precise fit of the old maidens, very woodeny-looking work, that any approach to a little more ease and grace was regarded as decidedly unneat. Beside, the staid dress-makers, with their neatness and obligingness, had some other traits which appeal very closely to the heart of a New England housekeeper—they were economical and honest. They cut a garment out of the very least cloth they could, and were willing to use their brains as well as their hands for their employers, in planning and saving. Then, they were honest. They always charged precisely what they thought the work was worth; never taking advantage of any extremity to turn a penny, and very often, in case of death in a poor family, making the entire mourning for nothing. The new dressmakers had proved themselves a little scheming —in short, our maiden aunts were good Christians, and that made them try every where, and under all circumstances, to do right; and the others knew little, and cared little for religion, beside having its name and its influence in a sober town like Mountford.

My readers will readily perceive that, though

not always sure to show its beneficial effects in precisely this way, true piety, in the end, is of incalculable advantage to us in our worldly prosperity, or, at least, so the aunts had always found it. It commanded for them the confidence of others, and that is what we must have in order to succeed; and the discernment by which even the irreligious learned to discriminate between these two kinds of piety in the rival dress-makers did not arise from any thing they said. The new dress-makers were oftener at meeting than the old, now they had the care of Tony; they spoke longer, and prayed louder, but, and here lay the difference, one acted the Christian perhaps in no greater matter than the sewing of a seam, or the change of a penny; while the others forgot that it is "these straws which show to the observing which way the wind blows," and did much of their work, with an eye-service, which was soon made evident.

To their surprise, the aunts found that, after a few days, Tony could take better care of himself than they could of him. He would sit for hours on the little braided mat (it used to lie before the parlor door, and had been too good for them to step on for years, but it was not too nice for the baby now), and play with bits of bright-colored cloths; or load the round basket with the empty spools, and trot after them as they rolled around the floor, with many exclamations of wondering impatience at their speed.

Like a sensible boy as he was, Tony at once seemed to recognize the fact, that the new occupation of his aunts had something to do with his future, and that he had better let them as much alone as he could. Occasionally, however, he forgot these good resolutions, if he had made any, and was guilty of some daring acts; for instance, one morning, when the aunts were busy hurrying through a new silk dress, they were suddenly called to cut and fit another, which they had promised for the day before, but the person with whom they had made the engagement had failed to bring it then; and, unused to saying "No," they left their work, and both going together into the kitchen, where things were not so scattered about, they became fully occupied and forgot Tony, and the dangerous place—among all the trimmings of the new silk—in which they had left him. Suddenly remembering him, Aunt Roxy exclaimed—

"What can Tony be doing to keep him so still?"

Rushing together into the sitting-room, there stood Tony by the table, busily engaged in tangling the last skein of nice sewing-silk. The buttons were laying about all over the room, the fringe was tied over and under the legs of the table, and the whole piece of ribbon, which had never before, in their extreme care of it, been unrolled, was twisted around the brass andirons, some of it so near the blazing wood as to be cracking and smoking from the heat, and some partly covered up with ashes. Pieces of the dress, looking as if they had been pretty well trampled under little shoes, were lying all around. What a scene it was to the astonished aunts! They looked from one ruin to another, with most woe-begone expressions, and then at Tony, who dangled the last skein of silk in his hand toward them, with a gleeful laugh, and the sweet child's wòrds—"Pitty! pitty!"

Aunt Cily was the first to recover herself; with a long stride, she seized the ribbon first from its dangerous position, and then they proceeded slowly, and with many exclamations of alarm and trouble, to rescue one thing after another, until the ruined heap lay together on the table.

All the time they were doing this neither of them had said a word to Tony; who, on the supposition that they had been collecting his playthings for his convenience, made a direct attack upon them, as soon as they came within his reach; but his hand was very quickly caught by Aunt Cily, who administered upon it the first real punishment Tony ever received. But now for the result. Instead of bursting into a loud, angry cry, as a child would, who was accustomed to being whipped, his lip trembled for a moment, the tears came into his eyes, and lifting the smarting hand, he said—

"Aunty Cily, kiss 'ittle Tony!"

Poor Aunt Cily! every trace of vexation vanished immediately. Lifting the child in her arms, she almost smothered him with kisses, using between them so many endearing words that any one, to have heard her, would have supposed she had been storing up the catalogue for years.

Aunt Roxy stood by, looking on with very moist eyes, and when Tony, once more at liberty, came to her for a repetition of the kisses, not unwillingly went over the same ground, taking care, however, to put in many loving shakes and ejaculations of "naughty, roguish boy," "and who do you think (kiss) is to pay (kiss) for all these things (kiss) which you have destroyed?" (kiss.)

Tony thought—of course, why shouldn't he? —that it was a great frolic, and would have been ready to have repeated it at a moment's warning, if, learning wisdom by experience, the good old aunts had not always been at much pains to put every thing out of his reach when they left the room. There are very few mothers whose love and patience would have come off as triumphantly from this test as did these maiden aunts. They restored such of the articles as money could buy back, and considered the affair, as in truth it was, more the result of their carelessness in leaving the articles exposed to the play of an active child, than as showing any moral delinquency on his part. Very strange it was in them, for are there not a great many mothers who are apt to meet precisely such an event as this with a heavier punishment than they would inflict for some sin? Any thing which makes them trouble, or care, or expense, it is hard, with these quick-tempered natures of ours, always to draw the line, and distinguish between what annoys us and what injures the child.

Not even all the kisses she had bestowed after

it, would wipe away from Aunt Cily's memory now the fear that she had acted hastily in inflicting that first blow. She mourned over in it secret, and strove to make amends to Tony for it, by innumerable little acts of petting and kindness, all of which, of course, served to make him quite mischievous and lawless.

While thus in a fair way to be spoiled by this over indulgence, Tony's religious education was not neglected. This was first in the estimation of his aged guardians, and they taught him, even before he had heard one line of Mother Goose, to say little prayers; never allowing him to shut his eyes at night until this duty was performed, though sometimes they found it so difficult to make him willing that, if they had any doubts upon the matter of native depravity before, they were all settled. Didn't they see it every night and morning in the way this little child turned away from his religious duties, and preferred to play rather than to pray?

Aunt Roxy generally took upon herself the

task of putting him to bed. One night, after an unusual game of romps with them both, she went through the whole process of finding the "five little pigs" as she pulled off his shoes and stockings, and really tired with the screaming and laughter through which he had passed, Tony crept into the crib which had, some time since, taken the place of the basket cradle, and, covering his face with the bedquilt, refused either to look out or to repeat the prayer for which Aunt Roxy stood patiently waiting.

"Come, Tony, come. Now I lay me—"

No answer. "Doesn't Tony want to say that pretty prayer to the good God way up in heaven, where his dear mamma has gone?" One would almost have thought the child remembered and loved his mother, to have seen what influence her name, used in this way, had upon him. Now one grey eye came from under the quilt, and it looked steadily in Aunt Roxy's face. "Say Now I lay me down," repeated Aunt Roxy; "that is a nice little boy."

"Now," said Tony, putting his face suddenly out.

"I lay me:"—"I lay me"

"Down to sleep:"—"Down to sleep."

"Well, little Tony, go on and say it all by himself, like a good boy."

"Good boy," repeated Tony, half shutting his little eyes.

"Oh no, Tony, that is not the prayer."

"I pray the Lord:"—"Pray the Lord."

"My:"—"My."

"Soul to keep:"—"Soul to keep."

"And—"

"That is enough," said Tony, resolutely shutting his eyes, and putting his head back under the quilt, "God knows the rest."

In spite of her "superior advantages," Aunt Roxy found her own voice was too unsteady to continue the conflict, so she tucked him up very closely and went back into the sitting-room, to repeat and enjoy the child's ingenuity with sister Cily.

"Surely there *never was* such a singular boy before; who ever heard of so many strange, smart speeches? What would he make one of these days, or rather, what was there in this world that he could not make if he chose?"

Ah, yes, this was one way in which God was answering the dead mother's prayer. She had asked that the little child might be made pleasant to those who had the care of him, so that they should be able to do for him from love, and not from necessity; and surely, never was a child more constantly loved and petted than this. Never one more in danger of being spoiled by indiscriminate indulgence. He had, however, one safe-guard, his moral nature; in so far as it was possible to separate that from their daily indulgences, was made a matter of special culture —I mean, he was early accustomed to receiving from the warm piety of the Methodist sisters a life-like idea of what religion was. It did not consist in a few forms; it burst from their lips morning, noon, and night, in some sweet, low hymn, which was in itself a prayer; it was there, in their patient, uncomplaining, faithful daily work; it was there, in their generous self-denials; it was there, in the solemn, hushed tones in which they read God's word, and offered their daily prayer. It had surrounded Tony from that first hour when Aunt Roxy stood rocking him with such awkward timidity in her arms; and, through God's grace, it shielded him from many a lasting injury which would otherwise have come to him from the want of any discipline in these early days. It would be very unjust to the natural order of things to say that Tony's character, so far as he had any, was not made to bring out and strengthen in his aunts, all those qualities of patience, forbearance, and gentleness, which are such excellent Christian virtues; but, while they did so, they often tried the dispositions, and wore upon the rather failing life and health of the sisters, so that they told in their fading and altering appearance, more tales of the lawlessness of their young charge than came to light in any other way.

People shook their heads, and said, long before the boy had thrown off his frocks, that "he would be the death of his old relatives;" but, fortunately for all concerned, they neither saw nor felt it. They only knew that those tiny hands had taken firm hold of their hearts; and though they were very experienced, and, in their own opinion, not lacking wisdom, still a little child did lead them. Poor, dear old aunts, that had to be coaxed into the slightest change, even in the pattern of a sleeve, for the last ten years, and now change and disorder seemed to run riot in their neat house; and, for some unaccountable reason, it did not matter, if only Tony did it.

So passed the first five years of Tony's life. He had pushed rather head-strongly through the intermediate stages of aprons and dresses, and now, came out arrayed in the full glory of a blue merino sack, plentifully bespangled with gilt buttons, and a pair of real pants, the first, made too, by Miss Jones the village tailoress. It was a very proud and happy day to both Tony and his aunts, when thus dressed, they led him into church. Tony, with his hand in each of his aunts, and his grey cap with the long tassel dangling on his cheek, very like the wing of a small robin.

Tony, of course, instead of listening to the minister,—Mr. White had gone now, and the new one had not the power of interesting children,—was busy all church time counting his buttons; and it seemed to some sharp eyes, that could not help watching them, that the more determinately Aunt Cily or Aunt Roxy pulled down his hands from the glittering row, or put their fingers on the red lips, so much the surer the sound came more audibly, "one, free, five, eight, whole heap of 'um."

"It was really very wrong;" so more than one mother thought. "Aunt Cily had always been finding fault with them about the way their children behaved, and here she let this boy disturb the whole church, playing off such pranks, and showing so much vanity. It was a sin and a shame, and they shouldn't wonder if it would be as well for them to pay back some of the good advice they had received with a little interest. Strange what folks were left in this world sometimes to do."

So Tony's new suit was the subject of as many remarks and scandal as some minister's wife's new bonnet; but fortunately its newness was as soon over, and before another Sabbath the sack and pants had become old things, and Tony was willing to earn the little "turnover" which he had been promised as a reward for well-doing, by sitting very demurely, with his great eyes fixed upon the preacher, until they suddenly closed, and he fell over into Aunt Roxy's lap sound asleep, and therefore very quiet through the rest of the service, of course earning the "turnover" when he went home.

It would be a great wonder if, under these circumstances, Tony should not grow up willful, selfish, and far too often, disobedient.

Every year, his aunts had said, "This is the

hardest year, if we can only get him well through this, we shall have an easier time the next." But now, as he was almost six, they could not help confessing to themselves that tangling skeins of sewing silk, hiding cards of hooks and eyes, tearing up the new paper patterns, and dropping silk buttons into such nice places, that they could never be taken out, were very trivial offences in comparison with not obeying them, with crying for the whole of a thing, and striking Janie Dawson when they wanted him to give her half of his apple; and worse than all, for fear of being sent early to bed, saying sometimes what was untrue.

In short, they found that the care of a child's body, and the watching over little annoying acts of mischief, ignorantly done, was a much lighter and very different thing from the care of his soul, and the watching over those intentional wrongs which he was now so apt to commit. They looked back with much regret to the past days of his babyhood, and heaved many a sigh for the times when their arms could keep him from all harm. They had such a feeling of helplessness with him now that of his babyhood bore no comparison to it. If it was not for the answers promised to the prayers of the dead, for the covenant blessing, they would be indeed discouraged, and yet Tony was only six years old.

It must not be supposed, that with their habits of thrift and economy, and their good sense, they were guilty of merino sacks overtrimmed for any thing but Sunday use. They made large, high-necked, dark calico aprons for every-day wear, perhaps a little too much from a girl's pattern to escape the criticism of those who were disposed to cavil at the endeavors of the maiden aunts in the line of mothers, but very neat and suitable, and quite to Tony's liking, until, on his sixth birth-day, he was, in accordance to his mother's request, sent to school. He had not been a week a member of Miss Turner's school before he came home one day without his apron, and being asked where it was, with much blushing and some stammering, said,

"Miss Turner told him to take it off and throw it away, it was so soiled."

Now, Aunt Roxy had put it on to him herself, very neatly washed and ironed, that morning, and therefore was quite at a loss to understand how it came "so soiled." She, however, told him "to go and get it, and bring it home:" but instead of obeying, Tony sat down on the floor by the door and began, as he was very apt to do when out of humor, to beat his heels and head upon the floor. There was nothing that made his aunts feel so helpless, for it always indicated an obstinate mood, in which he generally came off conqueror.

"Very well, Tony," said Aunt Roxy, in a cold manner, which she mistook for authority, "if you choose to lie there and kick your new shoes all out, you can; but I shall put on my bonnet and go right over to Miss Turner's after your apron. You are a very naughty boy."

Tony saw her put on her bonnet, and take down the large shawl, fold it with much care, and carry it to Aunt Cily to have it exactly deposited upon her shoulders before he stopped kicking, or broke the silence; at last, however, he said,

"Miss Turner don't know where it is, so you may ask and ask, and she wont tell you."

"I shall ask her, then, if she said it was so soiled that you must throw it away."

"I don't care if she didn't," muttered Tony, sitting up. "Tom Sanborn said it looked like a girl, and called me sister Suky."

"Tom Sanborn is a very naughty boy," said Aunt Roxy, taking no notice of his partial admission with regard to Miss Turner; "and he deserves to be punished for troubling little boys. I shall tell the school marm, and she will whip him."

This was evidently getting into rather deep water for Tony, so he stood up and made a step toward Aunt Roxy.

"Did he tell you to throw it away?"

"My name aint sister Suky," said Tony evasively, hanging his head.

"But your name is naughty Tony Starr, that wasn't man enough to bear to be called a foolish name, and threw away a nice, new apron, and—and—" Aunt Roxy's voice fairly trembled now, "told a falsehood to cover it up."

"I aint a girl," muttered Tony.

"You are not a good boy, either. Oh, Tony Starr! Tony Starr! what would your mother have said if any one had told her her dear little boy would live to tell a falsehood?"

"I did throw it away," said Tony, boldly.

"Yes; but did Miss Turner tell you too, and say it was soiled?"

"Tom said it was like a girl."

"That is a different thing. Come here, Tony."

Tony edged Aunt Roxy with that peculiar motion a child knows how to make, and while he appeared to go forward, he literally stood almost still

"Come more quickly, Tony, dear little Tony!" There was a gentle pleading in the voice then which seemed immediately to overcome all that was naughty in Tony. He ran with both arms forward toward Aunt Roxy, and said, as she lifted him up,—

"I threw it into the pond myself, way, way off, and Miss Turner didn't say nothing about it, only Tom kept saying 'sister Suky! sister Suky!'"

Now there was no use for Aunt Roxy to struggle against the temptation, she caught the child very close to her troubled heart, and instead of a lecture, or even a chiding word, gave him a series of loving kisses. There was one thing, however, which she did not forget or hesitate to do; when she put him to bed that night, she asked God, in very solemn and tender words, to forgive the little boy who had that day told a wicked, wicked falsehood—not to forget him through those long, dark hours when no one else could take care of him, because he was unworthy of his care and love, but for the blessed Saviour's sake, to forgive him, and to make him a great deal better boy for the future."

And Tony, with a troubled feeling about his heart, prayed after her, and asked "God not to send him away from heaven and his dear mother because he had told a naughty story about Miss Turner, and had thrown away his nice apron; but make him good, and not care anything about Tom Sanborn, and being called sister Suky, which was a great deal better than being called a liar, and sent for ever to the wicked place."

VI.

What Alice Clay did for Tony.

SUCH as we have been describing in the foregoing pages was Tony Starr, when he first went out from under the shelter of his kind aunts' roof, to mingle with other children. He was a queer, quaint, old-fashioned little boy, so different from the others that even good, kind Miss Turner, until she became accustomed to his odd ways, had hard work to restrain her smiles. As for the children in the school, it was a perfect holiday to them the first week Tony was there, for no one is more keenly alive to any thing which is not childlike than a child. Now, Tony did nothing as they did; he had an old-time way of holding his head, of moving about his ten fingers. The very motion of his feet was as if they were stiffened by age. His tones and words belonged to a generation gone by; and when he read in the reading class, though he was really an unusually good reader, as far as entering into and understanding what he read, still he pronounced his words so strangely that the taking up of his book was the sign for the whole school to be very attentive, and ready to laugh at the first mistake he made.

Tony took this all in good part; it was no stranger to him than every thing else was in this child's world; and he had far too much to observe to notice that he called nature *natur*, and said *eddication* for education, *sarvant* for servant, and a number of other mispronunciations, all of which the children were storing up to amuse themselves with, by and by, when they knew him well enough to tease him.

But it was not, unfortunately, only in these things that Tony differed from the others. He had been so scrupulously kept away from little folks, for fear of coming to harm, that he knew no more of their games and fun than he did of their manner of talking and acting.

He looked on, with as much wonder as he would have on a war dance, the first time he saw a game of "hunt the slipper;" and when they proposed to blind him, for blind man's buff, he stoutly fought the boy who came with the pocket-handkerchief, and persisted in his unwillingness until the fourth day of watching the game.

Of course there were in Miss Turner's, as there are in every other school, plenty of naughty children, who were very willing to tease and make a butt of him; and when they found that he was a quick-tempered, spirited boy, he really had to suffer more than he had during his whole lifetime before.

"Run for the ball, Tony!"

"Bring me that bat, Tony!"

"Halloa! here's Tony going to the moon!" and then some great, rude boy would toss him up and laugh when he came down hard, to see him rub his red, smarting hands. Then the boys played every trick they could think of, like making him take hold of a rope and pull, sure, when he was pulling the tightest, in compliance with their constant injunctions, to loosen their end, and then laugh when they saw him fall, as if it was a very good joke indeed. Before Tony had been in school a month, he was bruised and sore from head to foot, and what was of more importance, he began to feel irritable and cross whenever the scholars laughed at him, or repeated his old-time words after him. Now, if Tony had been a few years older, he had that in him which would have made all this of very little consequence; but he was not yet seven, and though his ways made him appear so much older that the others forgot it, yet he was easily discouraged, easily abashed, and not knowing what either feeling meant, showed his sense of them, by hiding away when any of the large boys came near him, and muttering his lessons over when called upon to recite them, as if he did not care whether he missed or not.

Poor little Tony! This was a hard time in his life, and he could not go for help where so many other children can if they are in trouble, for he had no mother; and though his old aunts were very kind, he never thought to go and tell them every little thing that annoyed or pleased him, as he would have his young mother if God had spared her; so after the affair of the apron he took a great deal of care not to say a word at home about any unpleasant thing which happened at school. He was tempted to occasionally, but he always remembered that it had once led him into telling a falsehood, and Tony had no wish to grow up an untruthful boy.

Miss Turner, after the first day or two, became quite used to his oddities, and he soon was nothing to her but one of the large number of children who came regularly to her for the six hours every day. She gradually as she could, without hurting his feelings, for she saw from the first that he was unduly sensitive, began to correct what was very old-fashioned in his pronunciation; but she left most of the peculiarities of his early training to correct themselves, through his intercourse with other children. She did not think what a hard discipline this would be for the little fellow, or she would have been kinder.

Before the term was half through, Tony became the butt of the school. His appearance was the signal for some "fun," as the boys called it, in which, I am ashamed to say, the girls often joined with as much apparent pleasure as the boys. Tony grew sulky, but never complained; he sometimes tried to laugh, and find in the joke the thing that made the others so much amused, but he rarely succeeded, though, do what they might, they never yet had made him cry, when they saw him.

As there were quite a number of boys in school of his own age, and even younger, if Tony had had any one to look after and instruct him in the ways of children, he would very soon have found his place, and kept it; but, for this first half term there was no one, and he was beginning to fancy he was not like other children, and to wish he might never be sent among them any more, when a new era opened in his life, for Alice Clay came to school. Now, Alice was a little girl only one year older than he was, and, like him, an only child; but God had spared her parents to her, and they were young, and very often to have seen the three playing together—one would wonder which was the greatest child. So Alice had grown up as much of a plaything as if she had had a dozen brothers and sisters; and as her parents were educated people, and had taken a great deal of pains with her, she was the "pink of perfection" in all those little matters where Tony was so entirely deficient; but what was better than every thing else in Alice, she was gentle, loving, and sympathizing, with a quick eye to see, and a quick heart to feel, what made another sad; and, therefore it was that, the half day on which she first came to school, was an era in Tony's life.

At the end of the very first recess, when, with a desire to "show off" before the new scholar, they had "put Tony through his paces," as Ned Baker called teasing him, and the little fellow, with flashing eyes and heaving breast, had skulked away the moment he was let alone into a corner by himself, Alice ran after him, and with tears in her eyes said, sliding her white hands into his,

"Come! I know where there are some very pretty flowers, pink and white, with long, slender green leaves. Mamma calls them 'fairy flowers,' but that is only to please me. They are not, really, you know; only they are pretty enough. You don't know how cunning they are. Come!" and she pulled away at the hand that lay very impassively in hers. It had never been held in that gentle loving way before, by another child; and the boy's heart answered to it in a heavy, dreamy way, like a tired baby just waking from its sleep. He sat still without making any effort to go with her, and so she said,

"Come! it is very near: I saw them as I came to school. You don't know how pretty they are."

Tony shook his head, but fixed his eyes steadily upon her.

"Don't shake your head so; you look so old you almost make me afraid of you. That is the way Grandpapa Grumbull shakes his head, but it never means no. So come, grandpapa."

Tony's lips drew together a little; he appreciated the fun of having *that* little girl call him "grandpapa," and he said,

"You may call me grandpapa, if you like, but don't let them" pointing with his finger toward the boys, "hear you; 'cause they will, too."

"Don't say them and caus," said Alice, laughing, "it sounds queer. Say—oh! say something else."

"What?"

"I don't know; that is wrong, I know. It wouldn't sound so if it wasn't."

Tony looked anxiously in her face and got up.

"That's a good boy," she said, very patronizingly. "Come."

Tony dropped her hand; he had a feeling of shame as he came in sight of the large boys with her, but they only called out,

"Ah ha! Tony's got a little wife so soon. Well, you are old enough to have been married twenty years ago,—did you know it?"

Alice stepped back, and put her arm around his neck, at which the children all laughed, and Tony would have shaken off the arm but he could not, it felt so pleasantly. So, in a few minutes, when they were out of sight of the group of children, his own found its way around her neck; and, for the first time in all these long, dreary, weary weeks, Tony Starr had taken a step into the child's world, and his guide was this winning little girl with her gentle love.

Tony came back with only a few spring beauties in his hand, but a new spring of beauty in his heart which should last long after the flowers had faded. He had grown younger every moment, as they hunted under and over the tall green grass,—Alice for the "beauties," and he all unconsciously for his lost child-life. It seemed to him, when he sat down again in that still school-room, that there was no one there but Alice, and that little bunch of flowers with their stems shut in a book-cover, and standing up in the corner of her red desk: he certainly forgot all about his book and his lessons, and when he went to his class made a poor recitation; so poor, that Miss Turner sent him back in disgrace to learn it over, and Alice looked, when he ventured to turn his eyes that way, as if she felt very much ashamed of him,—so at least he thought, though he did not otherwise care for the disgrace. But now he learned his lesson well; and when he was called up to recite it for the second time, spelt every word, looking full at Alice with a triumphant air, which seemed to say, "'There, you see I can if I only have a mind to."

After they were dismissed, one of the boys took Tony's cap, and flung it up on to the high branches of a tree under which they were passing. This was a trick Tony was becoming quite used to: but he was not behindhand in his ability to exercise any of the boys' natural gifts, like running and climbing; so he only looked up at it with a wonder as to how he should ever reach it, and sat quietly down to wait until he was left alone.

"Them's um," cried a boy, as he saw where it had lodged; "you'll have to stone it down as you would a possum, or you'll never get it over your wool again, Uncle Ned."

"That isn't my name," said Tony, stoutly.

"Oh, it isn't, is it! Well, Sister Suky then."

"Nor that either."

"What, none of them! You grow partikler, I sort of guess; it will be Jim Crow before you get hold of that cap of yours. Good-day."

The children laughed noisily; and after turning to throw a stone or two in a random sort of a way at it, the party all went on, and left Tony and his cap to his fate. Alice went with them a short distance, but turning round she saw Tony standing under the tree, looking eagerly up. The boy looked so small and the tree so high, that it immediately moved her compassion, and she went back to him.

"Can't you stone it down?" Tony heard some one ask, as he was intent on measuring the distance.

"No," he said, "I can't fire true enough."

"Can't you climb up?"

"I don't know; it looks very high."

"Try, and I will be here to catch you if you fall," and Alice stationed herself under the limb, and held up her arms toward it.

Thus encouraged, Tony made a vigorous attempt, but the trunk was so smooth and straight, and his arms were so small, they would not get hold of it: he only slipped back, scratching his hands and cheeks against the bark in a painful manner.

"Oh, dear! dear! you can't do it," said Alice, beginning to cry. "I wish my father was here; if you will stay here long enough I will run for him, he is on his way home from the office, and will stop at the next corner for me; he always does if he is first, and I wait if I am first, so we go home together. Don't tell," she whispered, drying her tears; "but mamma says I am his morning shadow, when they are little, short things on the ground—you know—and he is my night shadow, great, long ones, all stretched out, and ready to go to bed, and to sleep—aint that funny?"

Tony laughed, as if he really did not know whether it was or not. A father was a being he had only a very indistinct idea of in this world, so every connection with it was rather vague; but he saw Alice was pleased, so he wished to be.

All the time the children were talking, there hung the cap, nodding and bowing away to them, as the wind touched it, in a very absurd manner, they forgot their business was to get it down; and instead of any kind of trouble, they were having a fine frolic, when the village bell rung for half-past twelve, and they both remembered it was time for dinner.

"Oh, dear! dear! what will you do?" and Alice began to cry again. "You tie my handkerchief round your head, and I will really run for papa this time; I should not be surprised if he was most here, he often does walk way down here for me when school lets out late. You wait while I run up on the hill and look."

Alice ran away, and Tony watched her instead of the cap, as she went. Presently she turned round, took off her sun-bonnet, and waived it toward him, then turning, disappearing down the hill.

"She has gone," said Tony, very despairingly, looking in a sad way up to the dangling cap. "I'll fire at it two rocks, and then I'll try to climb up; and if I can't do it, why I must just go home bareheaded, and Aunt Cily and Aunt

Roxy, won't they stare and shake their heads when they see me."

So Tony gathered up his "rocks," very small ones they were; but, as he said, "he didn't know how to fire them at any object," and they came tumbling back, one hitting his head, and making him rather shy of any further attempts in that line. He next resorted, with a great deal of courage for such a child, to climbing the tree, but it was as useless as his stone-throwing, down he came, as soon as he was far enough up to insure a good scratching; and this time, so earnest he had been to "hold on," that the skin and blood came too. Tony looked all around, there, was no one within sight, so he put his smarting hands to his face, and began to give vent to the pain and the vexation in a good hearty cry. He cried out loud, a very unusual thing for him, but he felt so helpless, and, withall, so hungry; the time was going on—no cap—no home—no dinner—no body to help him. "Dear me," said Tony to himself, stopping his loud cries; "if I only had a father, wouldn't he flog those boys till they couldn't know beans, I tell *you*, I guess he would?"

"Well, well, my little man," said a voice close by him, as he finished his threat, "that sounds like a naughty boy, and my Alice told me she thought you were good. I am very sorry for you, don't get angry because the boys trouble you. See here, its only throwing up this stick, a light, smooth one, straight, right at it; so, and—there it is. Now put it on Tony, and don't let them get you vexed, so as to make you do wrong, because they are rude." And Mr. Clay took out his pocket-handkerchief and wiped the blood and the tears from the child's face.

"You've got some scratches here, off from that brown bark, I see; but never mind, I got a great many when I was as small as you are. Look up and see if you can find them now?"

Tony, who had hardly dared look up since Mr. Clay first spoke to him, now slowly raised his eyes, and saw a face way up above him, with some eyes very much like Alice's, only they were above a great pair of whiskers.

The mouth smiled down pleasantly on him, so did the eyes; and as he finished wiping off the dust and blood, and put the cap back upon Tony's head, Tony said, softly—

"Thank you, sir."

"That's right, you know how to be polite, and that is more than those boys know, I dare say, who threw away your cap. I hope you know how to be kind, and then never mind if they tease you now; the day is coming when you'll be a big boy yourself, then you can make them stand round; but even then you won't wish to flog them until they don't 'know beans,' shall you?"

"Yes, sir," said Tony, very decidedly.

Mr. Clay smiled. "Well, they deserve it," he said. "It's very mean to tease a little fellow that can't help himself, I would not give that," —and Mr. Clay snapped his fingers very significantly—"for a boy that would do it, would you, Tony?"

"No, sir," said Alice and Tony together.

"Then I will tell you what we will do now. We will vote not to think about it any more than we can help, while the scratches smart, and then, by-and-by, when we grow up to be big boys ourselves, we'll look out for the little ones, and if we see a great fellow tossing up their caps, where they can't get them, then we will just settle the matter for them ourselves, won't we?"

"Yes, sir," said the children.

Mr. Clay took a hand of each, and as his road home lay very nearly in the same direction as Tony's, they all walked together until they came to the handsome white house in which Mr. Clay lived.

There stood Mrs. Clay on the steps watching for them, and when she saw them, she said—

"What child have you with you to-day, Mr. Clay?"

"This is Tony Starr."

"Oh, yes; I have seen him often, but he is so

scratched up I didn't know him. How do your aunts do to-day, Master Tony?"

"Very well, I'm obleeged to you," said Tony, not at all abashed; for he had early been taught this part of his "education."

Mrs. Clay smiled. Why did every body smile, Tony wondered, when he spoke.

"Do you go to school?"

"Yes, marm."

"Do you like to?"

"No, marm."

"Why not?

Tony looked as if he did not wish to answer; and slipping his hand out of Mr. Clay's, said, "Good day," and started into a brisk run for home.

"What a queer little specimen he is," said Mrs. Clay, as she saw how nimbly he disappeared; "I have watched him very often when he has been with those old aunts of his, and always felt a great pity for him. I know they are very kind to him, but this education will

12

send him into life under a great many disadvantages, poor child."

"All disadvantages which he will overcome, if he has the real thing in him," said Mr. Clay, hopefully. "These are all external; the root of the matter, unless I am mistaken, is there. He has had the advantage of a good, prayerful home, and great watchfulness; they will tell in future times which these things wear off."

"Too much indiscriminate indulgence, I fear," added Mrs. Clay; "but do let us see if we can't do something for the boy, I can't help laughing at him. Why, he is as old as Methusalah."

"He never saw or heard anything else; if they have not indulged him too much, I will answer for him, so far as the instilling of good principles are concerned; but if they have, the boy will have a fair chance to be ruined for this kind of treatment that he must receive until he becomes more like other children, will sour him, make him not care, and ready, therefore, to do a great many wrong things."

"I hope not, but we must keep our eye on him ; remember, he is an orphan, Mr. Clay. It seems as if, when God attaches that name to a child, He set a great seal upon him, to make us see and feel the necessity of caring and feeling for it. Poor Tony Starr!"

So Tony went home from school to-day with, as we have already said, a new era opening in his life ; for to-day had brought to him some efficient friends, whom, the probability was, he would need very much before he grew to be a man.

Aunt Roxy was out at the gate, looking up and down the street very anxiously, as Tony came home. He had always been punctual before, and they felt sure something must have happened to him ; so they had spent the last twenty minutes wondering what it could be, and had taken turns to watch for him. When Aunt Roxy saw his torn face, her first thought was, that he had been quarrelling with the boys, and she looked very grave, indeed, as she caught hold of his hand and dragged him in.

Tony had no idea how he looked, so, of course, he could make no explanations; and the first thing he heard was—

"Cily! see here! Did you ever see such a sight in your life? What have you been doing, Tony Starr?—say, quick!"

"Nothing, Aunt Roxy, but climbing the tree after my cap; one of the boys threw it up, so I could not get it; I got some scratches instead."

Aunt Roxy saw the cap on his head; and now comes one of the results of having said what was not true, she did not believe him; but he looked up with a very honest face into her's, and said, as if he had understood her;

"Indeed it's very true; every word, Aunt Roxy."

There was something even then in the boy which prevented his saying, "You may ask Mr. Clay if I didn't." He felt as if he was telling the truth, and his aunt should know it; and so she did, after another searching glance, for she only asked,

"Who got it down for you, at last?"

"Mr. Clay, Alice's father."

"Oh, that is the little girl that we see going to church every Sunday, that looks so like a lady, and behaves like a lady. Well, I guess you aint been in any great harm if you have been with her, so come right along to dinner, here are your fish all fried up, crisp and nice, just your way, and a mug of milk, with the yellow cream all on," and Aunt Roxy held the brimming cup directly under Tony's hungry lips.

There it was, God's kindness to the boy showing itself even in this little thing. He had been hunted and troubled away from home, but it was home here, and the old aunts loved and cherished him as if he were the "very apple of their eye," and Tony felt it all as much as such a child could be expected to feel, what it indeed has hardly any other way of recognizing, but by some external sign, like the crisped fish and the creamy milk.

Before going to school in the afternoon, Tony

asked his aunt to sew an india-rubber band upon his cap, so that he could wear it under his chin, as he did when he was a " little boy," with which request Aunt Cily very willingly complied. Indeed, the old aunts were beginning very slowly to get an idea of Tony's real situation at school, and the result of a long afternoon's consultation was, that Aunt Roxy should go that evening, after Tony was asleep, so that he could ask no questions, and talk the whole matter over with Miss Turner. They had no idea what the true trouble was, neither could Miss Turner tell them, but they carried out their intention, and Aunt Roxy came home looking very sober and annoyed.

VII.

Tony's Trouting Excursion.

MISS TURNER, after the conversation with Aunt Roxy, for a few days, watched and defended Tony Starr. She spoke very decidedly when she heard any thing was going wrong. Reproved the children who were still inclined to laugh when he made a mistake, and from her window, behind her desk, saw that he was not imposed upon during the short recess. In all of this she was so ably seconded by Alice Clay, that after a short time, she gave the care of Tony up to her, and had the pleasure of seeing him, day after day, improve faster under her tuition than he had during the previous months. Indeed, he was becoming so boyish and rude that Alice, gentle and retiring as she was, was often at a loss to know what she should do with her protege, but before he became very troublesome, the care of him seemed to have passed from Miss Turner's hands and her own, into that of others who were very unfitted for it.

Nick Fisher and Lot Jones were great boys, twelve years old. They had been sent to Miss Turner's school with the hope that they might be kept, by the influence of good companions and a good teacher, from the evil courses into which young as they were, they had entered; but like all such boys, they were much more bent on getting into mischief than in getting good, though they knew enough of the strictness of Miss Turner's discipline to be sure they must conceal what they did that was wrong, if they wished to remain in her school; so all their plots were underhand, and of course only the more productive of evil.

As Tony Starr began to grow more like other children, they fixed upon him as a fit subject for their purposes, therefore, they began carefully, so as not to excite suspicions, to draw him under their influence. First, they took his part whenever any one teased him. Nick Fisher and James Warren had a "short fight," because James would keep Tony down on the ground when he wanted to get up and run off to play, and Nick got a black eye for his pains, but he was the first of the "big boys" who had taken Tony's part, and as the others were afraid of him, the effect was magical. Tony had not had so much real comfort in school since he came to it, notwithstanding all Alice had done for him, as he had the next day or two after the quarrel. He did not quite understand that it was on his account, but still he felt grateful to Nick, and was very happy if he would let him run after his ball, or do any thing for him, the rest of the day.

Having once established his character as Tony's "backer," as the boys called him, Nick took especial pains to keep it up. He made Tony quite a pet, and Lot and himself were not only ready to defend him every where and on every occasion, but they began to initiate Tony into boys' play; sometimes, little as he was, giving him the bat, and showing him how to use it, instead of always sending him after the ball, and sometimes giving him his turn at rolling the marbles, or knocking down the ninepins, instead of his being uniformly the drudge.

All this delighted Tony; as we have said, he was a true boy at heart, only he did not know how to show it. He liked Nick and Lot, a great deal better than he did Alice Clay; he had rather pitch quoits or wrestle than pick flowers or play baby-house. So he very soon forsook Alice entirely, and she, seeing him happy, and no longer persecuted, willingly left him with the other boys. In a few months Tony had passed through the various stages of initiation, and here he was, just after he had entered his seventh year, as noisy and rude a boy, among boys, as could be found in Mountford. To be sure he was odd and old fashioned still, but as he was large for his age, and mature in his ways of thinking and acting, he seemed more like ten than seven.

At first Nick and Lot made only a pet of him. They took him to walk and to fish with them, and though they were the occasion of his being tardy both at home and at school many times, yet no one seemed disposed to be very strict with Tony, and he escaped blame. These boys made him many presents. They gave him a knife, and a top, and a paper kite, with a long string, and made him a fishing-pole, all his own, with a nice pickerel hook attached to it, all of which made Tony very happy, and willing to do pretty much as they told him.

One Saturday afternoon they proposed a fishing excursion to a trout brook upon the sides of one of the neighboring mountains, from which Mountford derives its name; they were to go by themselves; though many boys asked to join their party, still they refused; the trout were a shy fish, and they wished no noise. As a great favor, however, they told Tony, he was "such a little chap the fishes would not see him if they tried, so he might go if he liked," and they would give him a trout hook and a fly. Tony had heard the large boys talk a great deal of this same pleasure of trouting, and he thought there could be nothing in the world quite so pleasant, but would his aunts let him? Tony's heart misgave him; he knew they were more afraid of running water than any thing else, and never once had allowed him to go near it, without one of them were with him, holding on very tightly to his hand. As for the sport of fishing, the kind old ladies had never heard the new theory, that fishes had no power of feeling pain; that God having designed them for food, had so created them that they could be hooked and left to gasp their last upon the dry banks of their home, without the least real suffering, although they appeared to have so much. I don't think they had ever heard that "trout are often caught with hooks in their mouths, which they have only carried off a short time before; or that bream might be packed in snow and preserved alive for a considerable time; or that carp had been frozen in a mass of ice so hard as to require an axe to extricate them, and yet they have recovered on being thawed;" or if they had heard these things, they did not believe them—not they; the possession of life was the possession of the power of suffering; and a fish was a fish, if it was a trout or a whale, and to kill them, unless in cases of emergency, was a sin and a shame.

Tony had always, from a baby, been made to love and care for every living thing. "The dear little flies" were companions and friends always. Mrs. Holt's kitten was a child embodied in a four legged form. Tom Low's puppy was almost an angel, he was so winning and pretty; and as for the birds, they were "God's choir"—so Aunt Cily said; and though Tony often thought how small they must look, up in his gallery on Sunday, he never doubted the truth of what he had heard. It was at school that he first saw a stone thrown at one of these singers, and he kept away from the boy for several days after, having a kind of fear that the bears would come out of the woods and eat him up, as they did the wicked boys in olden Bible times.

It was in school that he first began to lose his veneration for the fishes ; very slowly, but surely, the idea came into his mind, that to catch them "was fun," and those who "get the most were the best fellows." This thought of going on Saturday for his first fishing excursion was delightful to him. He was so absorbed in it, that he forgot every thing else ; he could not get his spelling lesson, and when he took up his slate to add his simple sum in arithmetic, he printed FISH on it, instead. So when he went home with his heart swelling with a request which he dared not make, he sat down absent-minded and a little fretful, when his kind aunt spoke to him.

There was no school on Saturday, but the boys, Nick and Lot, had work to do at home in the morning, so they could not go until one in the afternoon, and they told Tony they would wait for him by the meeting-house steps until five minutes after the clock struck.

All the morning Tony was busy devising ways and means to coax his aunts into compliance with his request; it did not occur to him for many hours, that he might ask them to let him go to play with the boys without telling them any thing more; but when it did, he immediately ran in with a very happy face, and not then a thought at his heart, that he was going to deceive them.

It was a beautiful afternoon; the light and shade played so invitingly on the near mountains, that, as the aunts looked out at them, to measure the distance, they did not wonder Tony wanted to go—they did themselves.

They inquired the names of the boys; and, unfortunately, did not know them, but to go to Miss Turner's school, seemed a pledge of their respectability; so with mamy private consultations, and much misgiving, they at last gave Tony leave to go until four o'clock, cautioning him over and over again to be sure and be at home then.

Tony was too delighted to realize that he was

abusing their kindness; indeed, I doubt if he could have told exactly how, if any one had taken him and tried to explain it to him. He could go, no matter about saying a word regarding the trout and the brook, and that it was not exactly at the foot of the mountain but a little way up, he could go, and that was enough.

Precisely as the clock struck one, he might have been seen running round the corner of the church with much haste. If after all he should be a moment too late and the boys had gone; but no, there they were, just coming through Mix's lane. They had their fish-poles in their hands; and now came to Tony his first distinct impression of doing wrong; he wished they would hide them in some way, so that his aunts could not see them as they crossed over the street. What should they hide them for? Tony Starr, why are you afraid to have them seen? If Tony had asked and answered these questions then, it would have saved him much after pain and repentance.

He had taken his own line and trout-hook, wrapped them up carefully, and stowed them away at the very bottom of his pocket. Ah, Tony! Aunt Roxy never meant that pocket, when she sat up so late, tired as she was, to make it, to be put to such a use.

The boys were surprised to see Tony, they had no idea the child would dare come without leave, and supposing he had, they avoided any direct question on the subject. They were glad to see him, for he answered two important purposes for them, he could bait their hooks after they had once taught him—he was quick to learn—and then, this was the chief reason why they had asked him, they could send him under the fence to pick that ripe watermelon on old Daddy Lawton's vines. They had been watching it for weeks, it was in its perfection to-day, and destined, as they well knew, for the Monday morning fruit stall, which the old man always kept, town-meeting days, by the side of the town-house. To say the truth, to pick and enjoy this melon in private, had been one great motive for the trouting excursion; their only trouble had been, how to secure it without exciting the attention or suspicion of Daddy Lawton or his dog Towzer.

Tony Starr was so small he could creep under the lowest rail of the garden fence, then if he crept along, the gooseberry bushes would hide him from view, and unless he made a noise so as to attract Towzer's attention, they felt very sure the melon was theirs; but how to prevail upon the boy to get it was a question. If children were as inventive for good as they are for evil, we should have a very happy world, but for some reason it seems always to be a great deal easier to bring about a wrong thing than a right. Perhaps it is because God gives them up for a season in order to show them how little trust they can have in themselves, or in any thing beside his grace, no one can tell; but certain it is, that when children have made up their minds to what they know they should not do, they almost always find a way.

After a little whispering together, Lot said to Tony, "Tony, down here at Lawton's, old Daddy Lawton's, you know, that cross old fellow that sits by the Town Hall when they have meetings, that man that looks so?" and Lot drew down his face, and made such an ugly grimace, that Nick laughed very loudly.

"I've seen him," said Tony; "he has lots of apples and pears on his table, and Aunt Roxy bought me a big orange of him once."

"Yes, that's the fellow; he always has candy and nuts, and lots of them things. Well, once Nick and I, we did an errant for him, and he told us, that the first real big melon that got ripe on his vines we should have it, so you see we have been on the lookout, and we found yesterday there was one ripe, a splendid fellow, *I tell you.* Well, now, you are along and will enjoy it first rate, so we have made up our minds to have it when you can get a slice of it, that will make your eyes open. We will point it out to you, and as you are the leetlest, all you'll have to do is to crawl in under the fence, grab it, and run with it as quick as you can to us, while we stay hid about the fence, so that no one else need see us and come and get it away from us; you'll find it as easy as nothing; wont it be comsplickum, say?"

"Yes," said Tony, jumping up and down, and rubbing his hands with much delight; "is it very, very big?"

"Quite a big one for such a little fellow as you are to carry," said Nick; "but here is my knife, it is as sharp as a razor, you just put it under the stem, and cut up so, and it will come off in a giffy."

Tony took the bright knife and drew it carefully across his finger, as if to test it.

"Look out there! it will go in before you know it, and you want all those ten fingers of yours to hold the melon; why it's twice as large as your head."

Now Tony had never tasted a melon in his life, and his eyes became very bright at the wonderful stories the boys went on to tell him about it. By the time they came near "Daddy Lawton's" he was all ready for the undertaking.

The boys had been up in the moonlight of the night before, examined the melon, and driven some low sticks down opposite it under the fence. They now described the spot very accurately to Tony, and gave him an old basket into which he was to put it the moment he had rolled it outside of the fence. In short, these wicked boys showed, by their manœuvers, that this was not the first time they had stolen fruit; every arrangement was complete, even to their entire security, for they took care to select their hiding place in a spot from which they could easily make their escape, if Tony was discovered.

Tony was quiet and intelligent in receiving their instructions; he did not even wonder at the excessive caution which they charged him so often to observe, for they had told him Daddy Lawton was up in town, and had left to guard his things his dog Towzer, but Towzer was so old, and blind, and deaf, that he would not hear him or see him unless he made a great deal of noise; and when they saw that Tony showed a little childish fear of the dog, Lot said,

"He saw Towzer go after his master before they turned down Willow Street, and it was only Marm Lawton, that was as cross as a fury, and would scold like every thing if she knew her husband had given away his melon without asking her." So Tony's fears all disappeared; and when they came to the place, with much celerity and dispatch, he obeyed his injunctions to the letter, and soon, to the boys' great joy, he was seen dragging the basket along after him, it being too heavy for him to lift.

"He's got it," said Lot, pushing aside the leaves from his hiding place, and peeping out.

"As true as guns I believe the chap has," said Nick, following his example. "It is a rum 'un for such a little chap, any how you can fix it. What would the old maids say?" and the boys looked at each other with much cunning in their ugly faces.

"Give me hold of it," said Lot, coming cautiously out. "Yes, that's the critter; you are the smartest boy in Mountford, Tony, and you'll make a man if you live to grow up."

"Quick!" said Nick, looking behind him over his shoulders; "Run with it, Lot, Tony can't go half fast enough with these short drum-sticks of his; clear away, cut dirt and run."

Lot laughed, tossed the basket up over one shoulder, and was soon out of sight, while Nick and Tony followed more at their leisure.

"Won't he wait for us?" asked Tony, in some trouble at seeing his treasure carried away.

"Of course he will, when he gets where it's shady; but you see, Tony, it aint no fun lugging that great thing along in the hot sun one moment longer than we can help; by-and-by I shall have a lift at it, but you shan't carry it any more, you have done your part, and are as nice a chap as there is out."

Now Tony had had so much of the other treatment at school, had been called so often "sister Suky," and "old woman," that it pleased him very much to be told he would make a man," and that he was "as nice a chap as there was out," he trudged along by Nick's side a very happy boy indeed, without the least idea that he just committed a theft.

As Nick had said, when they came to the woods where it was shady, they found Lot waiting for them. Lot's face was very red, and the perspiration was running down his cheeks, he had been working harder in committing this sin, than great, strong boy as he was, he would have been obliged to in order to have earned sufficient money to have bought the melon. But Lot had rather steal than work, even if he had to pay a great deal dearer for it.

Nick laughed at him when he saw him "puffing away like a pair of blacksmith's bellows," as he said, but Lot was tired, and that made him very cross, so he used some wicked words, which

Tony thought were not right, and for the first time to-day the child felt a little troubled, and wished Lot would stop.

It was now Nick's turn, covering the basket over carefully with an old pocket-handkerchief, he announced his intention of taking the matter as easily as he could, and the three boys proceeded slowly, but without half as much of what they called "fun" as they had when they started. Tony, too, began to be tired, it was a long walk for such little feet, much longer than he had thought. He asked Lot to set down a while and let him rest, but Lot was "out of sorts," and told him they had "something else to do, beside wait for him."

Nick, however, who was by far the best natured of the two, soon put down the basket, and throwing himself beside it, proposed they should "make sure of part of it, and lighten the load, by taking their first bite now."

Lot had no objections, so down the three sat upon the grass, and Tony, without knowing he was eating the "stolen bread in secret," thought never in his life had any thing been half as good before.

He was so warm, and so tired, that it was no wonder the cool, juicy fruit was very acceptable, and that when he had his share, he was more disposed to be still, and take a nap, than to go on.

As the boys saw how tired and sleepy he was, a new thought occurred to them, Tony would be now more "plague than profit;" they would rather bait their hooks themselves than to have him "dragging around." They would lie down too, and pretend to go to sleep, then he would "fall off;" and when he was "sound as a log," they would start away and leave him until they got ready to go home; then they would come back, wake him up, and thus be saved much trouble. So they told Tony they were going to sleep, and stretched themselves down beside him, and laid very still; but they only had to wait a few minutes, he soon gave evidence that they might go when they pleased without his

TONY LEFT IN THE WOODS.

knowledge; and so, after hiding all the water-melon rinds, they crept away, looking behind them, as long as he was in sight, to assure themselves that he did not move.

When Tony at last awoke it was quite dark, and his first thought was, that he was in his bed at home. He tossed his arms about, but instead of striking, as they often did, upon the side of the wall in the small bed-room, they came in contact only with the cold night air; thoroughly wakened by this strange sensation, he lifted himself upon his elbows, and began to look about him. He could dimly discern the trees waving their great arms over his head, and through them he saw the stars peeping down. Where was he? What did it mean? Tony rubbed his eyes violently, and, as he did so, very slowly the events of the afternoon came back to him, and he began to call loudly for Nick, and then for Lot. His voice had a strange hollow sound as it echoed from among the trees; so strange, that for some minutes he did not dare to call again, but, covering his face with his hands, tried to hide the great, queer things which were all about him. Then he felt cold and hungry, and every minute his fears grew stronger and stronger; he whispered Nick's name, so that if he was near him, he could hear, and as there came back no sound, he grew a little braver, uncovered his face, and sat up. "To whoo! to whoo!" sung a bird high up in the tree above him, and Tony said—

"Ah! ah! Mr. Bird, so you are here, are you; well, I know you at least, I've heard you on the Sodom apple trees a great many times. Can you tell me where Nick and Lot are?"

"Tu whoo! tu whoo!" answered the bird.

"Call away," said Tony, cheerfully, "I see how it is; they waked up first and have gone off after some trout, I am not going to be frightened at all;" here Tony's voice trembled a little, "but sit right up, and keep wide awake—and I thank you, pretty singer, for coming back to me. I don't feel half as lonely while you are there."

"Tu whoo! tu whoo!"

"Yes, tu whoo!—tu whoo!—tu whoo!" and Tony imitated the bird so exactly that the only wonder was, the bird did not think it was its mate, and fly down to him. It did keep on singing, very sweetly, almost as if it knew a little boy was under the tree, that was trying his best to be very brave and not cry, for some time, but at length it seemed to get tired, and away it flew. Then Tony felt very lonely; he ran up and down in the woods, in every direction, calling Nick and Lot, in a distressed manner. Every minute it grew darker and darker, and the stars shone brighter and brighter. Tony thought he had never seen so many before; he could not help wiping his tears very often, to see if they were all there; he felt afraid they would go away as the bird had, and then how dreadful it would be!

Tony grew stiff, and tired, and sick from the exposure of sleeping on the ground, his fright, and his loud crying; so he sat down again, and remembered the story of the babes in the wood, that Aunt Roxy had told him so often; he thought he was going to die as they did, and though he knew very little about death, he did not dread it. He looked about for a place on the grass, where the robins could see him easily, and he hoped they would come and begin to cover him up while he was alive, and could see them. Before he laid down he knelt, as he always did by his little cot at home, and folding his hands, said, in a loud, distinct voice, as his aunts had taught him was proper, this evening prayer :—

"Jesus, gentle shepherd, hear me!
Bless Thy little lamb to-night,
Through the darkness, be thou near me,
Watch my sleep till morning light.

"All this day Thy hand has led me,
And I thank Thee for Thy care;
Thou hast warmed me, clothed me, fed me,
Listen to my evening prayer.

"Let my sins be all forgiven,
Bless the friends I love so well;
Take me when I die to heaven,
Happy there with Thee to dwell."

Then Tony laid down, and sobbing for a few minutes, when he found there was no Aunt Cily or Aunt Roxy to kiss him; he said his prayer once more and fell again asleep.

Nick and Lot had wandered a number of miles away from the spot where they left Tony, much further than they had any idea of doing. They found many trout, and when at last their strings were full, and the sun had gone so low down that it began to grow dark in the woods, under the shadows of the great trees, where the brook ran, then they remembered Tony, and what a walk they should have back, before they could reach him. Nick felt very much troubled as soon as he found how rapidly it was growing dark; he thought the child had probably wakened, and if he had, he knew he would be frightened at finding himself alone in the woods, so he made more haste than Lot liked, and they both got some bad falls as they hurried over the slippery rocks, which did not tend to increase Lot's good nature.

"Plaguey little fellow," he said, "I don't see what we wanted to pester our heads about him for, we might as well have taken a six months' baby."

"Remember the melon," said Nick.

"Yes, but that aint nary here nor there, now its gone; and I'll bet a four-pence old Lawton will suspicion us, and be hauling us up, and the baby will let it out somehow; if he does, we shall catch it. My father told me he would flog me into an inch of my life if he ever caught me taking so much as an apple that did not belong to me; and he favors old Lawton, so there's no telling how it will end."

"Just like you, Lot; I never knew such a jackass. You are always for plunging head first into scrapes, no matter how bad, and then, when they are over, and there is danger of punishment, you begin to cry 'Don't, don't,—I will be good,' like any other whipt boy."

"Hold your saucy tongue, or I'll rap you over the head," said Lot, lifting his fishing-pole in a threatening attitude.

"Never you lift that pole at me in that 'ere way," said Nick, giving it a knock which sent both Lot and it reeling off from the stone on which he happened to be standing, in pretty deep water.

When he saw what he had done, Nick began to laugh in a very taunting manner; and Lot, trying in his anger to spring back quickly upon a stone and get hold of him, lost his footing and fell over once more into the water,—this time, in his efforts to save himself, losing his string of fish, which of course sank at once to the bottom of the stream. The water was not very deep, and was clear as glass, so he saw them lying very snugly down between two stones; but when he reached down to take them, he got hold of the wrong end of his stick, and, as he drew it up, they fell off one by one into the water, and the swift current carried them quickly away.

Nick, standing at a distance, saw the disaster, and judged it safe to beat a very speedy retreat; so, uttering a laugh more provoking than the other, he went off toward the spot where they had left Tony.

So much for the friendship between bad boys. It is well for us sometimes to measure it, and know precisely what it is worth.

Nick soon found himself tired, as he was running very fast. In truth the nearer he approached the woods the more alarmed he felt about Tony, and the more afraid of what Lot might do if he should overtake him. He needed to give himself no anxiety for the absent Lot, for no sooner had he gone than he, drawing himself slowly out of the water, made the best of his way toward home, without taking any further trouble about either Tony or Nick. Indeed he was so tired and cross that he was glad to be alone, and to make all the haste he could.

At last Nick came to the spot where, in the increasing darkness, he could only dimly discern the landmarks which he had left behind when he stole so stealthily away, to indicate the spot where Tony was left asleep. But to his dismay there was no child there. Hoping he might be mistaken, he explored the ground near; no other trees looked so naturally as those which he had first recognized. He had observed a curious twist in the lower branches of the pine tree just at their right, as he lay, with one eye shut, waiting for Tony to sleep. Remembering this, he felt rather than saw the tree, and there was the same twist but no Tony. Hoping he was mistaken, and knowing nothing was easier than to make such a mistake, he began to call Tony in a very loud and troubled voice; but Tony made no answer.

Could it be that the child had waked and gone home by himself? He would make sure that this was the place, then trust to the supposition and go back. It was not a pleasant place to be in for a bad boy. If all the birds in these woods had sung together, he would not have heard them. Children who have wicked thoughts in their hearts, have not a place for anything so pure and sweet as the song of birds ; and as for the stars that were so much company to Tony, it had been a long time since Nick cared to look at them. Now he heard the wind go sighing through the long, pendant, pine leaves, and he thought it said, "Daddy Lawton's after you—better go home." Then some great frogs began to croak in the still water close by him, and though he had heard them so many times before—one would have supposed he couldn't help knowing what they were—still, he had a fear when the note was unusually deep, that it was Towzer come to smell out the melon rinds which he had hidden away. He went to the spot where he had covered them up with stones and broken twigs, in order to satisfy himself that this was the place where Tony was left. He found it easily, though it was dark, and the rinds, too, just as he had left them. There was no longer any doubt, and as Tony was too large not to be able to take care of himself in an emergency, Nick began to feel easier, a little more sure that the boy had run home. Still, as he walked along, he stopped often, and kept constantly calling, "Tony! Tony Starr!"

When half through the woods, whistling as noisily as he could to keep his courage up, he happened to remember that the week before, when he was lounging around the steps of the tavern, he heard two of the mountaineers discussing the weight of a large bear one of them had killed on this very mountain, early in the spring, when he was out in the woods "maple-sugaring." This, Nick knew, was no very uncommon occurrence: he often saw a large black bear brought down to be sold for meat before the door of the market house, but he had entirely forgotten it. In the day time there is very little danger from these animals, for they seldom have been known to attack any of the human species so near a town, though they commit great devastation among the sheep and calves; but in the night, or when lying still and exposed, Nick knew they were very dangerous adversaries. He tried to keep on whistling, but he could not bring his lips together, they were so stiff from fright. What if Tony had been eaten up, and the bear, having a taste of boys' blood, was hidden in some covert, ready to spring out and devour him as he passed. His teeth began to chatter from fear, and his knees trembled so that, instead of being able to start and run, as he so much wished to, he could but just draw one foot along after another. O, how dark and dreadful the woods were! He did not hear any longer the rustling of the pines; he was too intent on peering into every thicket, for the great glowing bear's eyes, to think of any thing else, excepting now and then, when a dry limb crackled with a short, quick sound, as if an animal were giving a sudden bound forward. Then Nick felt as if he should fall to the ground, and indeed, he did so nearly several times, that he lost his string of fish, and was soon as badly off as Lot himself.

In one of these stumbles, Nick felt sure the object over which he fell moved, and when he darted back, in great alarm, to avoid it, a child's voice, said softly, "Aunt Roxy!"

"Tony! Tony!" whispered Nick, not much above his breath.

"What," said Tony, dreamingly, "good-night, Aunty."

"Oh, Tony Starr!" exclaimed Nick, "how glad I am to find you. I was afraid the bears had eaten you all up."

"Bears!" repeated Tony, fairly wakened by the dreadful word; "Where? where?" and he began to cry.

"Oh, nowhere, I guess," said Nick, very much reassured by finding the child alive and well. "How came you way off here, I should just like to know."

"The little birds were coming to cover me up, as they did the babes in the wood, and I thought I should be dead," said Tony.

"Dead? you are good for a hundred years yet. Never knew any of them robins cover up such a big boy. Come! those aunts of yourn will be tired wondering where you are, and we shall have the whole town out arter us," and Nick pulled Tony on to his feet, and without stopping to answer any of the many questions which he was continually asking, kept tight hold of his hands, and walked with long strides on through the woods.

It was strange what a different feeling boy Nick was, when he found Tony alive and well. Very much of his fear of the dark and the bears seemed to vanish; he began to whistle again, until Tony said, "Please don't walk so fast, Nick, my feet ache so and my knees, I can't keep up with you?"

"Can't you? well, its a proper long way off from home yet, and I am as hungry as a meat axe. Catch hold a little tighter, and I'll kind of drag you along."

Tony literally obeyed, but the "kind of dragging" was not such a pleasant operation. Sometimes it knocked his feet so hard against the stones that it drew from him a sharp, quick cry of pain. Sometimes his arm seemed as if it would come off at the shoulder, Nick pulled so fast; and Tony thought it was a great deal pleasanter waiting with the stars in the woods for the birds to come, than walking so. He put his lips firmly together, and tried very hard not to cry; and the more tired he became the more unceasing were his efforts not to be a baby. Nick at last became conscious what an exertion he was making, and said, kindly:

"'Taint no matter to kill ourselves to get home a half an hour sooner. The mischief's done with them aunts of yourn; so we will sit down and rest us. There is the end of the woods; when we get there we shall be close by the road, and, may be, we shall get a turn with somebody. That's a man, hold on a leetle, just a leetle longer, and if there aint no other way, why I'll get you home on somebody's wheelbarrow; great fun, wouldn't it be? to ride, with me for your bay mare? I tell you, I would go it."

Tony summoned all his remaining strength and courage and stepped forward briskly to the point toward which Nick was going.

Yes, there was the road, and a large flat stone by the side of it, looking, in the star-light which shone down very brightly, now they were out of the woods, as if it was placed there on purpose for people as tired as they were to sit down and rest; and down they sat, weary enough.

Tony would like to have gone to sleep again, and sat up close to Nick, laying his head on Nick's broad shoulder.

"No, down here," said Nick, making as soft a place as he could on his knees; "you may fall off a little, while I listen for a wagon."

Now Tony had only an idea that "falling off" meant tumbling down from the rock; so he clung to the boy with his little hands, not knowing that by this very action, he was appealing strongly to all the good there was left in him; but he did. And Nick, that hour, under that star light, with the orphan child nestled so close to him, had a vague wish come into his heart, that he was a better boy; that he hadn't sent Tony to steal the melon; that he hadn't pushed Lot off into the water, and then laughed at him until he made him so angry. It was a very indistinct feeling; but after all, this is the way God very often speaks to sinners, and it is what the Bible calls, "His still small voice." Nick half listened and half turned away, as if he was ashamed of it, and shouldn't like to have Lot, or even Tony himself, know exactly how he felt.

Tony soon breathed loudly, and moaned with a sad kind of a moan, as if he was sick or unhappy, Nick could not tell which. He did not like to wake him, so he sat still wondering what he could do, and thinking he would give every thing he had in the world, if he only had not brought Tony with him. The melon, certainly, "had not paid."

Down upon him twinkled the stars. Nick looked up to them, and, big boy as he was, he felt as if he should like to ask them, what he should do, with a fancy that perhaps they might answer him. Whether he did or not, he never told; but pretty soon he got up, took Tony softly in his arms, and started to carry him home. He went forward very bravely for a short distance, but Tony was almost a dead weight, it would not do; he put him down so suddenly that Tony screamed with pain and fright, and clung quite wildly to Nick. At this moment Nick caught the sound of approaching wheels. "You shall ride any how," he said aloud, and began to call very vigorously before the wagon was in sight.

Pretty soon, however, a gruff voice answered, and Nick found to his dismay, it was Daddy Lawton returning from having put up his booth by the Town Hall. He stopped his horse as he came opposite the children, and inquired again what was wanted, and when Nick told him that he wanted a ride for little Tony Starr who had been fishing and got lost in the woods, the man said :

"Wall now, that's curous, how things cum abeout, I was just goin' in to that very house arter my wife's new gown. Jump in! jump in! you are both on ye welcome to a ride ; but who *are you*, tother fellow there? seems to me I don't know your voice, and it is too dark to get a squint at you."

Nick felt very much inclined to give some other name, but Tony was wide awake, and he knew that would never do so, he said "Nick!"

"Not old Nick, I hope," said the man, laughing ; "but jump in, there aint no time to waste."

Nick put Tony in on the straw in the back of the wagon, then jumpt in after him, and without asking any more questions, the man whipped up his horse, and away they went.

Was there ever anything so resting? To be sure the wagon had no springs, and came down with a jerk every time it passed over an uneven surface, but what did that matter, a coach and six could not have been more luxurious to the tired children. Tony did not keep awake even to enjoy it, he gradually became heavier and heavier as he leaned against Nick, until he tumbled down once more, or as Nick said in a whisper to Daddy Lawton, "he was done for."

As soon as they came into the village, Nick stepped out without asking the man to stop, or as much as saying "thank you;" he had his reasons for wanting to get off as unobserved as he could, and when Mr. Lawton looked around to speak to him, there was only Tony rolled up like a ball on the straw.

In a few moments after entering the village the wagon stopped before the door of the maiden aunts, and Daddy Lawton saw by the unusual flitting about of the lights, that there was quite a commotion within—and so in truth there was, as the reader may readily suppose.

From the moment the clock struck four, one of the aunts had been stationed at the window watching for Tony. As one hour after another passed, and he did not come, their trouble, alarm, and at last, consternation, may be imagined. Neither of them dared to leave the house to inquire for him, for fear some word would come during their absence, of harm having befallen him, which would require them there; so they walked up and down from the gate to the house until it was too dark to see any longer, and then they carried lights from one room to another about as rapidly as they had paced the walk, looking out from the windows of the house to every different point of the compass. Sometimes they were weeping, sometimes they were praying, and at last, when the clock struck nine, and nothing had been heard or seen of Tony, unable to bear it any longer, Aunt Roxy went over to the minister's and consulted with him what to do. He had returned with her to the house, and before making any commotion in the town, had proposed to ask the assistance of God. They knelt for a short, fervent prayer, which was hardly finished before they heard the sound of wagon-wheels stopping before their door, and in a minute, Daddy Lawton made his appearance, with Tony still sound asleep, in his arms.

For a time no inquiries were made; it seemed to the aunts such a direct answer to the good minister's prayer, they were awe struck into silence; taking Tony from Daddy Lawton, Aunt Roxy went again to the chair at which she had been kneeling just before the wagon stopped, and said, briefly,

"Will Mr. Alden unite with us in giving thanks?"

Simple and touching were the thanks, during which the aunts wept freely, uttering their fervent "amens," and signalizing this event as the one great occasion for gratitude of their whole lives, while unconsciously the orphan boy slept on, hearing none of these holy words, but notwithstanding, while he dreamed, behold there was a ladder set up on earth, and the top of it reached heaven, and behold the angels of God ascending and descending on it.

VIII.

How Nick came in the Sabbath-School.

THE next morning Tony was not questioned very closely by his aunts respecting the events of the afternoon. It was the Sabbath, and they aimed to impart such an entirely sacred character to its hours, that Tony should, from his earliest childhood, remember it as holy. Nothing secular was ever allowed to intrude. The very toys and books which littered the room on week days, were exchanged for a few which could only convey an impression of sanctity.

Tony was given a Noah's ark, because the story of Noah was a Bible story, and a variety of Sabbath-school books, and cards, took the place of the gay-colored weekly ones, with which the fondness of his aunts liberally supplied him.

When he was very young, Tony liked the

change, particularly as he was never allowed the ark on any other day, and then, too, his aunts sang a great deal to him, and would talk more with him, and dressed him, taking him to church where he saw so many other children; but as he grew older, and began to prefer real animals to these small wooden ones, and story books, with a good deal of adventure in them, to the memoirs of children so pious that they were far removed above his sympathies; then he began to think Sunday was a dull day, and to wish it would not come so often. As soon as he showed this spirit, his aunts became more strict with him, they took away every thing that could interest or amuse him, and made him sit still in his chair, and learn an additional lesson in the Bible, after he had committed that for the Sabbath-school. If he rebelled, which he did very frequently, then they added a hymn, and made its perfect committal a necessity, if he wished any of the usual Sunday favors.

Of course all these things did not answer the

end intended, and many a beautiful Sunday,—these were always the days on which Tony was the most rebellious, the aunts went to meeting with aching hearts, while little Tony trotted along beside them, looking very sour and discontented, and not at all as if he thought God meant this to be the very happiest, dearest day of all the seven.

It was for these reasons that Tony, to-day, escaped with very few questions; for when he began to tell his aunts about the water-melon, and how nice it was, they immediately stopped him, with,

"Tony! Tony! do you forget it is the holy Sabbath; we don't talk about melons and our worldly pleasures on the Sabbath. You may repeat the ten commandments."

"I don't want to," said Tony, kicking the table legs by which he was sitting. "I should think if there was anything wicked about a water-melon, God wouldn't have made them grow."

"Tony Starr, there is nothing wicked in the melon; you know that is not what I mean, but in talking over our worldly plays in holy time."

"That wasn't a play," persisted Tony, "it was only eating. Why don't you say so about pie or cake, or bread and butter? So, aunt, I don't think its wicked a bit. I hate Sunday; I can't never do or say anything then but its always wicked—wicked—forever wicked."

"Oh, Tony! Tony!" said Aunt Cily, holding up her hands, "what will God do to you—you frighten me. Repeat the fourth commandment immediately, and see what He says; and you naughty, wicked boy, say you hate Sundays! Oh, Tony! Tony!"

Tony was melted a little by the evident pain which he was giving his aunts; he looked up from under his eye-brows with a peculiar expression he had, when he was just beginning to be sorry, and said—

"Pooh! Aunt Cily, don't make a fuss about it. I can say the fourth commandment a hundred times if you want me to," and then, in a low voice, he muttered it so carelessly one would have been at an entire loss to know what he was saying, if they had not been accustomed to his rather self-willed way of doing things.

"That will do," said Aunt Cily, as he finished. "Now I hope you will ask God to forgive you for having said such a wicked thing; and never —never, as long as you live, do it again. You will learn to love the Sabbath, above all other days, if you are ever a good pious man."

"Its so still," said Tony; "and you don't, let me ever say a thing I want to. I don't like any days when its meeting time always."

"But don't you know, Tony," said Aunt Roxy, "that if you ever go to heaven its always Sunday there; don't you remember the hymn says:

"Where the assembly ne'er breaks up,
And Sabbaths never end."

"Then I don't want to go there," said Tony very decidedly. "I had rather go to school, and have recess and play hours, a great deal."

"Oh, what a wicked boy you are, Tony! sit still on that chair, precisely where you are, and don't you open your mouth again until you have learned this hymn—this precious, beautiful hymn on the Sabbath. If you can't talk without saying such naughty things, you shall not speak again to-day," and Aunt Roxy placed before the child a well-worn hymn book with this hymn:

"Welcome, sweet day of rest,
That saw the Lord arise!
Welcome to this reviving breast,
And these rejoicing eyes.

"The King himself comes near,
And feasts His saints to-day;
Here we may sit, and see him here,
And love, and praise, and pray.

"One day amid the place,
Where my dear Lord has been,
Is sweeter than ten thousand days
Within the tents of sin.

"My willing soul would stay,
In such a frame as this;
And sit and sing herself away
To everlasting bliss."

"Think of that, Tony," said Aunt Roxy, as she finished reading the hymn, in a clear, really melodious voice.

> "One day amid the place,
> Where my dear Lord has been,
> Is sweeter than ten thousand days."

"Ten thousand days, Tony, that is a great, great many—of pleasurable sin."

"What is that?" asked Tony, looking up very brightly.

"Why doing wicked things that give us pleasure, but are sin."

"Like eating a water-melon?"

"No, Tony, no; there was nothing wrong in eating the melon, and God made them on purpose for boys like you to enjoy. What is wrong is talking about it in holy time; it isn't 'the holy frame,' the hymn tells us about."

"Sing it, please Aunt Roxy," said Tony, coaxingly.

So Aunt Roxy began to sing it to a sweet tune, in which Aunt Cily immediately joined;

and Tony, with the book in his hand, followed them, to their great satisfaction.

"Again," said he, as soon as they closed. "I like these kind of Sundays, when you sing with me, and tell me stories."

The sisters looked at each other, and immediately recommenced. "Dear Tony; he was quick tempered, and very often said things for which he was sorry. Was there ever a better boy than he was now, sitting there with that hymn-book in his hand, singing with them like an angel?" so Aunt Cily whispered to Aunt Roxy in between the chorus of these hymns.

As they went into Sabbath-school that noon, Tony saw Nick standing squeezed in behind the door of the vestry, wanting to speak to him as he passed. When he was near enough, Nick put his head down close to him and whispered—

"Not a word about the water-melon to any one, if you don't want to catch a flogging."

Tony looked frightened, and drew up closer to

Aunt Cily, who, turning round, saw Nick, and said kindly to him—

"Come, little boy, come into the Sabbath-school; you shall have a nice book to carry home and read, if you will."

Nick hung back a little further behind the door, but if he had chosen a place in which he could be easily caught, he couldn't have selected a better one; and no one was a more indefatigable seeker for Sabbath-school children than Aunt Cily.

"Come," she said, "come in to-day: I have four boys in my class just about your size, all good boys, too. Come, you shall have a very nice book to take home."

"I guess I won't to-day," said Nick, at last finding his voice; "I am in kind of a hurry."

"A hurry, Sunday! Oh, I wouldn't be; you'll find you'll get through all you have to do a great deal better for keeping the Sabbath pretty strict. I found it out a great while ago."

"Do come," said Tony, taking hold of Nick's

hand; "you'll like it, I know. The lessons are real short, and the singing is very nice."

"No, thank you," said Nick, making up a face at Tony.

"Oh, yes you will!" said Aunt Cily. "I thought you would," and she pulled the door open. "Now Tony, lead him right into my class."

At the same moment she opened also the vestry door, and Nick found the eyes of all the school fixed upon him. To pull away from Tony and run, was his first impulse; but the minister at that moment caught sight of him, and calling his name very loud, asked him to enter.

Nick saw that the best thing he could do was to go in as if he had always intended to; so, looking very sheepishly, he allowed Tony to lead him, and soon found himself sitting with eight other boys in Aunt Cily's class.

As we have before said, Aunt Cily was a very good teacher. She had a way of giving life and interest to every thing she talked about, and it was no wonder,—the Bible was a living book to her, full of great and beautiful truths. These words of a hymn were to her, as if some one had gone down into her heart, and transcribed them from thence:

"I love the volumes of thy Word!
What light and joy these leaves afford
To souls benighted and distressed.
Thy precepts guide my doubtful way,
Thy fear forbids my feet to stray,
Thy promise leads my heart to rest."

Aunt Cily never but once had a child join her Sabbath-school class and leave it voluntarily, and that was more than many others can say.

Nick had never been in the Sabbath-school before. He had heard it spoken of among the children, but he always thought it must be a very stupid sort of a place, and one he would not be caught in. Indeed he seldom went to meeting on the Sabbath. He had not been inside the church to-day, only hanging around the steps so that he might have a chance to speak to Tony as he came out. He had no idea of listening to a word that was to be said, any more than he would have had if he had been going into church. But Nick never remembered that God was there, and that, if his Spirit touched his heart, he *must* listen.

The lesson happened to be on the parable of the prodigal son, and though Aunt Cily did not know much practically about wicked people, yet it was not difficult for her to imagine what kind of a young man he was. So she depicted his character in very graphic words,—told the boys just how he was probably living when he determined to "arise and go unto his father." She repeated over and over several times, the very words he intended to use when he spoke that first dear word, Father, after he had spent all that his parent had given him in riotous living, when he was so poor and miserable that he envied even the husks that the very swine were eating: yet he could come back, and could use again that precious name, father.

The boys all, even to Nick, had their eyes fixed on Aunt Cily now, for her voice was trembling as she spoke: "Father, I have sinned against heaven and before thee, and am no more worthy to be called thy son; make me as one of thy hired servants."

The boys had many questions to ask as she proceeded. Some wanted to know what the husks were, if they were like our corn husks here; and another asked if the swine were like ours. Then they wondered how much was paid the hired servants, and they wanted to know about the kind of money used in these countries, and how its value compared with ours; and so, what with questions of this kind, and their teacher's own remarks as to the character and sins of the prodigal son, they were not half through this short parable when the bell rung for the lessons to be closed.

Nick was sorry; he wanted to know whether the young man went home, and if he did, what his father said to him. He looked round at the clock, and saw to his surprise that they had been engaged forty minutes. Why a sermon forty minutes long seemed so long, how could it be that there was such a difference.

When Aunt Cily handed him a large book, he read on the back " Horace and May," and opening it saw it was full of pictures, he thought this was a very different place from what he had supposed it to be, and he shouldn't wonder if he tried it again, particularly if he came once, to hear the rest of the story of the prodigal son. The other boys, too, all seemed so glad to see him; and when they were going out Seth Fowler gave him a push, and said, " Old chap, I'm glad to see you here. We've got the best teacher of the lot, not one of them that can hold a candle to her, if she is as old as the hills, and an old maid too."

" Lor', Seth, I got catched or I shouldn't have been here, I tell you; but I like your schoolmarm up to clover, and I dare say I may come again."

" You had better. I always get a book that's

worth a day's hard work, and so will you; only she is mighty particular about your bringing it back, and taking good care of it."

Nick handled his a little more carefully. "If you come next time you may have mine. It's 'Now or Never.' You'll like it first-rate; all the fellows do. So you had better come."

Nick thought, perhaps he should. So he said, "Well now, done. Keep that for me, and I'm in for it, lesson or no lesson. But say, Seth, do you know what that father did when the wicked son came home? Did he hire him, or did he turn him off? The way my father would have told me to tramp, would be a caution, I say, for it."

"Don't you really know, Nick? What a heathen you are! Why, my mother taught me when I was as high as your knee."

"But my mother never teaches me such things," said Nick. "So I keep out of mischief and do my work, is all she cares for."

"Well, I wish, if I could spare her, you could borrow mine for a spell. Why, if we never have any other learning, I tell you what, we shall know all about Abraham, Isaac, and Jacob, as if they were our first cousins."

The boys were now some distance from home, and had come to the point from whence their paths lay in different directions; but Seth called after Nick so loud that many heard him, "Hold on now until next August, and then we are going to have a great time at camp meeting; you won't be sorry if you do, I know."

Now, Nick had heard something of these "great times" before. They consisted in a sort of Sabbath-school celebration, in which those of the scholars who had recited the most perfect lessons, been most punctual, and learned the greatest number of verses, received a prize, consisting of some good books, a handsome Bible, or something of that kind, and Nick, who was fond, as all boys are, of occasions, had long had a secret wish to be in some way engaged in one; so this only made him the more willing to think of going, and he said,

"Well, we will see when the time comes."

The next morning at school Nick very soon sought out Tony, and asked him many questions as to the way in which his aunt had received the story he had to tell about the trouting. He was very much relieved to find that they had hardly made an inquiry; appearing to feel perfectly satisfied with the fact that he was home safely, and the determination they had formed of not allowing him to go again. Nick cautioned him over and over, not to say a word about the melon, or their having left him asleep, assuring him if he did, beside "beating him," they would "never let him go with them any where again as long as he lived."

Tony, without knowing what he did, promised to be very silent, and as Nick and Lot both knew he was remarkable for keeping a promise, they felt quite assured that their theft would never be discovered.

Finding Tony so easily taught, and, as they said "cute," on this occasion, they took many opportunities, soon after, to use him for their own purposes, and it was astonishing how alert and cunning, for a good boy, Tony was.

The habit of petty pilfering was one in which these boys indulged to a very great extent. They seldom took any thing as large and expensive as the rare water-melon, but almost every day they managed to appropriate to themselves some little thing which did not belong to them. In this habit they very soon learned Tony could be of the greatest assistance to them. They would take him into a store, perhaps where a barrel of apples would stand open near the counter, and tell him, before they went in, to pick out two or three of them, and put them in his pocket while they paid the man for them. They would then step boldly up and talk with the man, while Tony would take and secrete the apples—one apiece, at least—and then they would run off and enjoy them together.

Sometimes they ventured on a thing of more importance, and by some cunning excuse, would make the child take and bring it to them. He being so small, and so well known as the charge of the good Methodist sisters, that no one thought of suspecting him.

Poor Tony, it almost seemed as if he could not be under worse influences, and what made them more dangerous, was the fact that they were of such a kind, that neither his aunts nor himself had the least idea how sinful and destructive they were.

Nick and Lot managed not to have Tony too much with them before those people who were well acquainted with them; and as Nick, since the Sunday he first went, had been very regular, and a good scholar at Sabbath-school, it completely blinded Aunt Cily as to his real character.

Nick boasted to Lot that "he only went to make the old lady believe he was a saint, so that she would let Tony alone."

Of course Tony could not be so much with these bad boys without both seeing and hearing a great deal that was wrong, and to come daily under such influence must tell very powerfully upon his character. To be sure he did not understand a great deal of the real guilt of what he was led to do, but there is a certain unconscious influence which comes from evil, that taints and colors every thing it acts upon.

Tony began to use bad words, at first carelessly, because he heard them so much, and was quick to imitate; and then soon, because he saw they made the large boys laugh, and he thought it must be smart; and, at last, so quickly grows a bad habit upon us, because he did not know that he did.

When he was at home he came naturally into his usual course of home life; he never thought of saying what was not proper before his aunts, and so Tony had begun to bear the reputation of being a bad, profane boy before they had a suspicion that he was anything but their "good little Tony."

Before he was nine years old Tony was never

missing, if there was mischief going on, and was apt to be among those who were the most forward in the petty wrongs, which boys are careful not to call sins, but which are sins, in the pure eye of the clear-seeing God.

Now, although a great many knew that Tony was getting into bad ways, no one went to tell his aunts. Some were afraid it would "almost kill them," which was a very mistaken kindness, indeed; and some said, "The old maids might know if they chose; none were so blind as those who wouldn't see;" while the majority shrugged their shoulders and coldly remarked, "So much for giving a child to be brought up by those who know nothing about it; anybody, with sense, might have seen what would come of it. The boy was going to the gallows as fast as he could, and if the town did its duty by him, it would send him to the House of Correction with as little delay as possible. It was all that would save him." Poor little Tony Starr! is there nothing else left for him? what has become of that treasury of prayers, and the dead mother's legacy; surely, God, too, has not forgotten his promise to the orphan; and yet the child seems going on to his ruin, both here and hereafter, without a hand outstretched to pluck him as a "brand from the burning." Even Alice Clay shuns him, rude and wicked; he has nothing in common with her now.

IX.

True Kindness.

TONY'S ninth birth-day was a great event with his maiden aunts. Eight long years since the dying mother put into their arms that little baby, and here he was now, a great, healthy boy, every one else would have added that dreadful word, wicked, to the list, but his aunts were still in almost entire unconsciousness of the fact. Tony had learned many bad things, which crept out day by day, more and more, and which often made his aunts wonder what they could mean; but he was generally obedient and quiet at home, and then, by some mysterious arrangement of Providence, the affection of those who have the care of children, seems to blind them entirely to what is so obvious to every other eye. The very first real suspicions the aunts had of Tony's character came from his running away two Saturdays in succession from school. Miss Turner, hoping to enlighten them, had come both times, on her return from school, to inquire if he was sick, and had found, as she anticipated, that he had left home, saying, he "was going to school." Tony had an excuse all ready, when he was found out, and his aunts' eagerness to know where he had been, prompted them to make the inquiry so soon that it left him no time to seem to have intended to deceive them. He had "been sent by Mr. Clay on an errand," he said, "which had taken him all the morning," and he produced a ten cent piece, which he had given him in payment.

This was a good excuse; Aunt Cily put the money in Tony's little tin "missionary box," and as the boy listened to its rattle among the other small bits, a verse of the Bible came into his mind, this is the wages of sin, and the Bible says, "The wages of sin is death." "I wish it was out of there, the rest is all good missionary money, and this will spoil it."

He had some conscience left still, and God is now speaking to him, for he has been guilty of three wrong actions, and they come up before him, more and more distinctly, as that money rattles, rattles, louder and louder; it almost seems to him as if he could distinguish it from all the rest.

He has played truant from school; he has been with a party of bad boys over to Cromwell to see a cock fight; he has bet on a large game cock and has won these ten cents; and he has told a direct falsehood to his aunts to cover it.

Oh, dreary prospect enough for the young parentless boy! His aunts trust him, and do many kind things, as if they would obliterate from their own minds the suspicion they have had; at any rate, they will be very careful that it does not wound him; but when the very next Saturday, quite delighted by the ease with which he has escaped now, he plays truant again, and again says that Mr. Jenkins sent him to carry a bundle over from his store to

Parson Brown's, at the other end of the town. Then the aunts looked at one another, and a doubt crossed their minds, whether that child, looking them full in the face, is not saying what is untrue. The doubt remains with them after Tony has gone away again to play, so that Roxy, dresses herself in her Sunday best, and goes down to Mr. Jenkins' store to inquire. Mr. Jenkins, of course, has not seen him, and does not know what she means, and he takes the opportunity to say, "These boys need a pretty sharp look out, Miss Roxy, I have one about the age of yours, and he is oftener in a scrape than out; he tells me Tony is pretty fast; I shouldn't trust him farther than I could see him, if I were you, watching wont hurt him any way."

Aunt Roxy went out with a very heavy heart. Tony had told a falsehood here, there was no denying it, perhaps it would be as well if she should just step over to Mr. Clay's and inquire about that other Saturday, and the ten cent piece. So as she was "all dressed up," Aunt Roxy called at Mr. Clay's door, and it always seemed to her afterwards, that God sent her as directly as if he had commissioned an angel to come visibly down from heaven and lead her there. Mr. Clay was not at home, but Mrs. Clay was, and she had been wishing for some time, that she could in some way have access to the ears of Tony's aunts, for, from the first interview with him, when Mr. Clay came leading him home by one hand, and Alice by the other, she had felt an interest in the child, which had made her watch with much anxiety and pain, his downward steps.

Aunt Roxy was too intent upon learning the truth to yield to any delicacy which at another time might have prevented her asking what she so much wished to know, she came to the point without any preamble, and Mrs. Clay met the question as frankly and as freely.

She "had not heard Mr. Clay speak of having sent him away, she had no idea that he had; it would be very unlike him, to take a child from school for any such reason, and she was sure he would never have done so without asking permission of the child's guardians." Then Mrs. Clay went on to say, "she was very sorry to hear Tony was so constantly in bad company;" here Aunt Roxy gave a start, which made her sure this was news to her. "There was no safety for so young children but with those who were wiser and better than themselves—a fatherless boy had always seemed to her more exposed to temptation and sin than any other human being."

Mrs. Clay spoke kindly but firmly; it seemed to her that God had delegated so much of the care of the child into her hands, and she did not mean to be unfaithful to her trust; and Aunt Roxy only interrupted her with short prayers and some very deep sighs. After Mrs. Clay had, as she thought, thoroughly opened Aunt Roxy's eyes, she began to comfort and assist her, and indeed, that trembling, fluttering, failing heart, had need of it all.

While they were conversing, Mr. Clay came in. He said, of course, that he had not seen

Tony on that Saturday, and should never have thought of doing such a thing, as employing him on any errand, without leave; but he did more, he offered to see Tony now, and find out where he had been then, and with whom.

At first Aunt Roxy looked alarmed at the proposal, she did not know what punishment he might inflict upon him, but Mr. Clay, reading her fears, promised her to deal very gently with the child, but thoroughly, as it seemed to him his future good depended upon a decided, efficient course. He knew "the evil that was in the the world" better than Mrs. Clay, and the possibilities at which she had only hinted, he stated as certainties, in strong, glowing words, so that Aunt Roxy bent under them like a broken reed, nor would he be restrained by the imploring looks which his wife from time to time cast toward him.

"The truest kindness," he said, in reply to her expressions of regret, after Aunt Roxy was gone, "is to be thorough, honest, and true with them now, or they will lay up sorrow enough to bring their gray hairs very quickly to the grave."

Aunt Roxy tottered home, as if she had been stricken by the hand of palsy. Many who noticed her as she walked along the streets, said: "How fast Aunt Roxy fails; that boy will be on the town before long." But no one saw her without a feeling of sympathy and sorrow for her. The aunts had a firm, deep hold on the affections of the people of Mountford; they had lived too good, pure lives to have it otherwise. Aunt Cily was much alarmed, when she saw her sister's pale, woe-begone face. She read the truth of their suspicions in her first glance; nor was she as wholly unprepared for what Roxy had to disclose, as her sister had been to hear it, for she had spent the time since she had been left alone, in following out some awakened trains of doubt, and she was by nature, shrewder and keener than her gentler sister. She heard the recital with a firmness and resolution, which did more towards sustaining Roxy than all the comfort Mrs. Clay had offered; and fully believed that the best thing for Tony was, to leave him to Mr. Clay; and while they were very watchful, not to begin by finding fault, and making home uncomfortable to him.

Mr. Clay knew enough of human nature to be very sure, that with their anxieties made keenly alive to every fault of Tony's, the aunts would be in great danger of driving the boy into desperate courses, rather than aiding him in keeping away from them, by continual fretting and worrying him at home.

He argued rightly, that no boy of any true spirit, will bear the constant fault-finding which is apt to be characteristic of a woman's discipline; he knew that the strong, bold, "must," or "must not," of a man, was more easily and pleasantly yielded to, than the "please don't," or "you naughty boy, how can you," even if the one prevented his doing what he wished, while the other only retarded him.

His stringent advice therefore had been, that

one only of the aunts should make known to Tony that they had become aware of the deception he had practiced, if he choose to confess where he actually had been so much the better, but if not, then leave him to him.

Mr. Clay had been, as well as his wife, interested by what Alice had told him of Tony, and also by what he had himself seen on the day when he had rescued the cap; but it happened rather strangely, he had never seen Tony where he could talk with him since he had heard how wicked he was becoming; he felt sure he was worth the saving, and that in Mr. Clay's opinion was what very many of the boys in Mountford were not. He had among his other theories, one, that if a child at an early age becomes vicious, he becomes so radically lost, that he never can be of any real use in this world, and can at last only be saved, as by fire; but Tony had, as he had once said, "the root of the matter in him," and every excuse for the wrong turn he had taken, in the peculiarities of his home life.

As Aunt Roxy, from all the vividness of the impressions which she had received abroad, was more excited than Aunt Cily, it was obviously best that the task of fault-finding should devolve upon Aunt Cily; therefore, after Tony had gone to his room—the neat new room, which they had had finished for him as he grew to be a large boy, in their attic—Aunt Cily followed him, and Aunt Roxy as she listened in breathless expectation down stairs, heard Tony's voice in all moods, but knew at last that he was broken down and was promising amendment, for he was sobbing while Aunt Cily was praying. Aunt Roxy sobbed and prayed too, and so closed upon them the evening of Tony's second known delinquency, and so the Sabbath morning found them, for they both sobbed and prayed more than they slept, until the gray dawn came.

Mr. Clay, in accordance with his promise, took the earliest opportunity of deepening upon Tony's mind whatever good impression he might have received from his conversation with his aunts.

He found the child, more tender and truthful than he had anticipated, and what gave him more hope than any thing else, he was not, as so many children are, ready to promise all and a great deal more than is asked them, but he only said, when Mr. Clay told him of the two courses of life which were open before him, and that he was already choosing between them,

"I will try, sir ; I had rather be good."

And so Tony really meant ; but, to be good was so difficult. Tony had no idea it could be. He struggled very manfully against all the temptations which came for the first few days. Resisted every inclination to join the boys in what he knew was wrong, and did not utter a wicked word, *if he knew it ;* but poor Tony, he was already suffering from one of the most speedy punishments God sends upon sin—an unconsciousness of committing it—that is, he said these wicked words without knowing that he was going to, until they were spoken.

The boys all noticed the change in Tony, for

children are very apt to see and feel quickly what often entirely escapes older and more blunted faculties; the good ones were pleased, but the bad were annoyed, and made their minds up, one and all, that Tony Starr was too useful and too merry to lose, so they would get him back, as Nick said, "by hook or by crook."

His aunts ventured Tony much more seldom away from them, than they had done. On holidays they generally contrived some amusement, which should keep him at home, or take them with him, and then Mr. and Mrs. Clay were indefatigable in their exertions in his behalf. They planned to bring him often to their house; and though Alice shrunk from him now, he was so rude and boisterous, still she was willing to amuse him if her mother would stay near; but generally Mr. Clay took him with him to his office, or sent him with his gardener, Joe Pearson, on an excursion where he could get nothing but good. Fortunately, Joe took a great fancy to Tony, and said, very often, "that there warn't a fellur within ten mile that could whip that little chap when he got a year or two more on his head. Let him alone now, and they'd see if he wouldn't make um stand round like one o'clock, one of these days."

Nick and Lot grumbled very much over this new order of things, and, as I have said, were busy maturing plans to counteract it. One which after some consultation they had devised, was to make him ashamed of his aunts. They thought if they could get him to feel that they were rather to be despised than loved, they should soon undermine their influence; and as there was no one else to exert any positive authority over him, they should have him at their disposal again. So they began to say all manner of saucy and wicked things about "pious old maids," but not to Tony, only so that he could hear them.

Tony for many days did not appear to understand or take any interest in their hints, and very likely their trouble would have been all thrown away, had not a smaller boy one morning, when he refused to do something he wished to have him do, repeated some of Lot's speeches, joining them in a very taunting manner with his aunts' names. Tony became very angry, and he threatened to "flog" the little child in such a determined way that he was frightened, and easily made to ask his pardon, though he did it in an impudent way suggested by Lot:

> "I beg your pardon, I crave your grace,
> I hope the cat will tear out your face."

The boys laughed very boisterously, and Tony, went away feeling down-hearted and ashamed. He wished he had whipped the boy; he wished his mother was alive, and his aunts were young and handsome; he wished, from the bottom of his heart, he wished it wasn't such hard work to be good.

The little boy, Bill Stevens, quite delighted with his success—for it always seems success to a boy if he can make his companions laugh—the next day came with some more rhymes, which Lot and he had made as they walked along to school together, so that Tony, when he came into the school-yard, where the boys were all sitting around on the ground and on stones was saluted with—

> I'm Aunt Roxy's only boy,
> I'm Aunt Cily's darling joy.
> Sing high, sing ho!
>
> My old-maid aunts are tall and thin,
> Shingles without, soft soap within.
> Sing high, sing ho!

Tony stopped, and the blood mounted slowly, as it did when he was very angry, into his face.

"Sing that again, if you dare to," he said, throwing off his cap, and, small as he was, placing himself in the attitude of an experienced fighter.

Lot and Bill began, but none of the other boys opened their lips, they already felt a sympathy for the little hero before them.

Without waiting for them to finish the first line, Tony approached them and hit Lot a hard blow, directly in the mouth.

Now, Lot was much taller, and almost twice as strong as Tony; he had never dreamed of his venturing to attack him; he thought if he fought at all it would be with Bill, who was so much smaller, that, to punish him, would have been comparatively easy; he was wholly unprepared for the attack, and when he felt the stinging pain which the well-directed blow occasioned, he sprung upon his feet like an angry dog, and flew at Tony as if he would tear him to pieces; but Tony, for a moment, stood his ground bravely. Lot was, however, far too strong for him, and he soon had him down, and was beating him unmercifully, when Nick, who happened at that moment to come into the yard, interfered, and the other boys coming to his assistance, Lot soon changed places with Tony, and lay bruised on the ground. Tony gave him a few parting kicks in right, good earnest, then ran, as Nick advised, to hide himself under Miss Turner's protection in the school-room; but what a looking child he was. His face was black and blue in many large spots, and the blood was dropping from his cut ear, and from his nose. Miss Turner sent for water, then rang the bell, and ordered every child to their seat, though it wanted ten minutes of time for school to begin. Lot came in, and his appearance at once showed he had been the other combatant. As soon as Tony had washed off the blood and dirt, she told Lot to do the same, which he did unwillingly ; indeed, nothing would have tempted Lot into school, but the fear of his father, and the certain punishment which he knew awaited him at home, if he ran away.

When the boys were more in order, she called them up before her, and made a minute examination into the particulars of the case. This ended in her expelling Lot, without any hesitation, from school ; and disgraced, smarting with the blows which he had received, and dreading the additional pain which awaited him at home, he slunk out from the schoolroom, and away from among the boys, so many of whom he had already injured.

Miss Turner could not find it in her heart to blame Tony, indeed she rather looked upon this ready and generous defence of his aunts as a harbinger of good; so she contented herself with telling him he had better go home, and remain there until his eyes which were red and swollen, were in a better condition for study.

Tony reluctantly obeyed; he dreaded the remarks and pity his appearance would call forth. He did not see how he could tell his aunts that the boys were laughing at them, and that was why he fought them. He walked part way home irresolute and fearful, and every moment of hesitation his dread of the meeting grew stronger; at last it quite overcame him, and turning, he ran swiftly to the place which he was already beginning to regard as his asylum, Mr. Clay's office.

Without waiting for the formality of a knock, he pushed open the door, and said—

"Mr. Clay, see how I look, sir; I don't dare to go home."

Mr. Clay was very busy, but he could not help being startled, as in the black and blue boy before him he recognised Tony Starr.

"Why, Tony!" he said, "what have you been doing?"

"They sung some poetry about my aunts," said Tony, reddening with anger; "and I told them not to do it again, but Lot and Bill did, and, as Lot was the biggest, I hit him as hard as I could in his mouth; then he got me down, and I don't know but what he would have killed me, if Nick had not come and saved me; but I don't care anything for the beating, Mr. Clay, only my aunts. I don't want to tell them how the boys were laughing at them. Should you, sir?"

"Why no, Tony, I think not," and Mr. Clay pushed away his papers. "Come here and let me get a nearer view of you. You look more like the pictures I have seen of a boxer after a prize fight, than like any thing else I can think of."

Tony stepped close up to Mr. Clay, and held up his bruised face in a very confiding way.

"This is a bad business," he said; "but we will talk more about it another day, when the external and internal smart is over. Now we will go home to Mrs. Clay; she is a good deal of a doctor—perhaps she can do something that will make you look a little better."

Mr. Clay took the shaking hand of the child in his, for Tony was still trembling from excitement and anger, and holding it very firmly, talked to him about other things until he had the pleasure of feeling it grow still and warm in his pressure.

Mrs. Clay could not do much—fighting boys were out of her line; but she continued the process which her husband had begun, and by the time his aunts would be expecting Tony home, he was in a much fitter condition to go, particularly as Mr. Clay went with him, and said "that Tony had got into a quarrel with a large boy because he said some impudent things about them, and had got some bruises, but he hoped they would forgive him, for he had promised him to try and never strike a blow when he was angry again."

Tony listened to him with much delight, while he had an undefined idea that he had done something that was not quite right, he also felt very sure that neither Mr. Clay nor his aunts blamed him as they had when he had been guilty of other sins, which had not left any mark on him externally. He was rather puzzled, and during the week which followed, before he was able to go again to school he spent much time trying to think it out.

The worst effect which followed from this was, the disposition which the children showed, when he went to school again, to make a hero of him. Now there was nothing to which Tony was so susceptible as flattery. He could not be driven, he could not always be coaxed into doing what he did not wish, but he could almost always be flattered.

Nick very soon, by a little well timed flattery, backed as it was by the memory of his late defence of him, began to regain the influence he had lost, and before Tony had the least idea that he was again easily yielding to temptation, he was "hand and glove" with Nick and his associates.

There was, however, one thing now in his favor, Lot's father, discouraged by his expulsion from school, had decided to send him to a farm of his brother's, who, not having any children of his own, had often written to him for one of his boys. Lot was the only one that could be spared,—no one ever wants the care of such a child if they can avoid it,—so Lot's trunk was packed, into it his mother dropping many tears; and he went west.

If he had remained, Tony would have been, for the present, at least, safe; but the very worst part of the mischief seemed to be taken away, now Lot was gone. Nothing so wicked was proposed, and there was less quarrelling and profanity, so Tony was doubly in danger. He yielded one thing after another, until he began to run away when he saw Mr. Clay coming near him, and grew cross and often impertinent at home, in short, Tony was a backslider, and that only a very little time after his aunts and Mr. and Mrs. Clay were beginning to hope he had turned over the leaf, upon which was to be written the new, better life.

X.

Opening the Legacy.

BEFORE Tony Starr had reached his tenth birth-day, no one doubted in Mountford that he was ruined. Even Mr. Clay was forced to give him up, for he could not find any way of getting hold of him. Tony avoided him when he met him unexpectedly, and if Mr. Clay sent for him to come to his office, always refused. Miss Turner had been obliged to give notice to his aunts, that unless he changed his course, she could not retain him in her school; and the poor aunts themselves, constantly thwarted in every attempt to govern him, or make him do what was right, were literally going, as Mr. Clay had predicted, bowed down with sorrow to their graves. They "faded as doth a leaf;" their voices were no more heard leading in their sweet, clear way, the social psalm-singing; if they attempted to do so, they broke down into almost inarticulate quavers, and they gave up, by degrees, one after another of the meetings in which during their long lives, they had taken so much enjoyment; but as Mrs. Simmons remarked, "one prayer they made now, was worth a dozen from common people, they were so subdued and heavenly like," and so they were. Suffering always brings us near to God, and if we are near, we shall hold communion with him in the earnest simplicity which shows we feel and mean what we say, and this is always sure to meet with a response.

It seemed very strange that a little child like Tony should have the power of so affecting two lives, not more intimately associated with his; but it must be remembered how keenly they felt the responsibility when they took him, and how dearly and unexpectedly they had learned to love him.

Suffering as they did now in health and spirits,

they were of course unable to pursue their trade with their usual industry and success, though they changed their spectacles much oftener, still they could find nothing that would enable them to "make button-holes, and do the nice stitching." People began to complain that their fitting was not in the old style, they very often made mistakes, and some too serious to be remedied. It was very sad, but the fact was undeniable, the maiden sisters were growing old so fast that they were rapidly becoming unfitted for their work, and as they had drawn largely and generously upon the resources which they had laid aside for this dark day when it should come, during Mrs. Starr's illness and death, they were now failing in health and in ability to help themselves, without any where to turn for aid. It is not surprising then that they thought with much interest and curiosity of Tony's Legacy, which had never been taken from the Bible since the day, nine years ago, when Aunt Roxy had sewed it up. It was a frequent subject of discussion between them, as they sat thinking darkly over their own and Tony's future. "Suppose it should be a gift of land, which had risen during these years to an almost unprecedented value." Such a thing was not uncommon, many instances had been told them of similar fortunes unexpectedly realized, and should it be so, what a kind providence it would be to them now. Tony's birth-day was to be in June, beautiful, sunny, leafy June, and the hope which the very glad summer time seemed to give, lent its influence to a degree of which the aunts were not conscious, to their thoughts and plans. The story of the legacy had been carefully concealed from every one, not even Tony knew what was awaiting him, but as the time for the tenth birth-day approached, the aunts thought it would be better to take Mr. Clay into their confidence, because if the lands were at all involved with the property of other people, it would be necessary to have the business in the hands of a lawyer who understood it. The communication was therefore made, and the surmises of the aunts seemed to Mr. Clay not improbable, particularly as Tony's mother had fixed the opening of the legacy at so early a date, in order, he thought, to meet precisely the emergency which she had foreseen might occur in her aunts affairs. Sincerely hoping for their sakes that it was true, Mr. Clay proposed that the paper should be opened on the night before Tony's birth-day, in order that they might know whether it would be best to tell him what it contained. They were all very decidedly of the opinion, that if it should make him wealthy, the knowledge of the fact should be withheld strictly from him until he was in a better moral condition to receive it. Beside, as Mr. Clay remarked, "if it should be property in western lands, it would doubtless be best not to part with any more of it than should be necessary now, as every year it would rise in value. Discretion was very necessary in order to manage every thing so that it should result to the greatest advantage to the child, and it might be, that they should decide to have the whole remain, as it had for so long, a profound secret. At any rate, it should do so until the legacy had been read."

The last day of Tony's ninth year it really seemed to his aunts as if he intended to show how bad a boy he could be. He spent the morning in Mr. Capon's lime kiln, a very bad place for a boy, for the kiln was worked by wicked and intemperate men, and when he came home at noon he brought with him sure evidence that he had been in close contact, to say the least, with the two vices of drinking and smoking.

When his aunts reproved him, he told them very plainly that he was "tired of being forever scolded that he thought he was the worst treated boy in Mountford, and that he intended to run away."

That same afternoon he disappeared, and terrified by his threat, Aunt Cily went to consult with Mr. Clay. He said, nothing was more probable in the moral condition he was, than that he might attempt the thing, but as he was small, he could not walk very fast or far, on the first day, and could be easily traced. He advised that nothing be done about finding him until his absence into the evening should make them feel quite sure of his intention, then, he promised to be himself answerable for his recovery and return.

What a heart-broken afternoon that was to his aunts. They walked up and down the small rooms, looking out of the windows with their anxious, tear-blinded eyes, hour after hour, their whole souls intent on seeing the boy on his return home. But no; the afternoon passed slowly, oh so slowly, and no Tony. It began to grow dark, and Aunt Cily went up to Tony's room to see if there was any evidence of his intentions there. Strange they had not thought of it before, but it is so hard to do anything which will confirm a suspicion that injures those we love. The upper drawer of the small bureau which they had bought for him was half way open; and out from it, in curious confusion, came knots of all kinds of colored cords, bits of tin, nails, torn tails of kites, fish-hooks dangling on their broken lines, leaves of writing books,—in short, all the et ceteras which compose a boy's treasure house. Aunt Cily had often made ineffectual attempts to put this "to rights;" so she knew better than Tony himself what it contained. She pulled it wide open now, and looked it carefully over. There had some of the most precious things been taken away. A knife, which was his father's, and which they were keeping until he was a man, and therefore only allowed him to carry on great occasions; a small pin ball in the shape of a heart, the very last sewing his dead mother had done, and the story of which they had so often repeated to him; two lead pencils, also his father's property; and a pocket Testament out of which he had learned all his verses since he could read, and which he had insisted on keeping in the "sacred corner" of this little drawer. These things were undeniably gone. Aunt Cily called her sister, and they hunted in every imaginable place, where they could have been secreted, but they were not to be found. Not an article of clothing had been taken, not even one of the new shirts with linen bosom, which Tony had coaxed his indulgent aunts into making, and which had been, of all his wardrobe, his pride and boast. The aunts looked at each other in a speechless, hopeless dismay, and read in their pale and altered faces without the need of words the realization of their fears.

Mr. Clay called as they finished the search, to see if they had made any discoveries and to open the Legacy before doing any thing further. He consoled them in some measure by telling them that he had already track of Tony, and had no doubt that an hours' driving would bring him back to them.

In preparation for the great event of opening the Legacy. Aunt Roxy had made the parlor tidy, as she said, which meant dusting it over every hour of the afternoon, and had drawn the table with the small solar before the sofa, placing upon it the neatly tied bundle. Nine years, nearly, had now elapsed since she put on that cord, and took, with more than her usual dress-make precision, those small stitches; how sacred it had been, never forgotten, and the curiosity over which she triumphed with so much difficulty at first, always in full force, whenever her mind was turned towards it, but still inviolate; there lay the package now as it was those long years ago.

Her hand trembled with eagerness, wonder, doubt, hope, and expectation, as she laid it by the family Bible. What might it not contain for that wandering, wicked boy, who, to-night of all nights of his life, should be here, and was out under the stars, no one knew where or for what purpose. Did Tony's mother see him and see them to-night? if not, who were the ministering angels, and what did it mean, that they were sent to do God's bidding? In a case like this, with that wealth of promise for the faithful parents and the remaining only child, if God forget him and them now, if that mother forget them, where could be their hope? when, and how, would God "take him up?"

It must not for a moment be supposed that the aunts made all these preparations without many half uttered prayers, many fervent ejaculations for help and direction. It seemed to them that they had nothing left but prayer; no aid that could really avail them, but what come to them from their Almighty friend. If there had ever been a half day of their lives when they felt the presence and sustaining power of God too, it was to-day. "As thy day so thy strength, Roxy," said Cily, with a heavy sigh, "if we had been told a year ago we should ever come to this, neither of us should have been here to-day to have seen this Legacy opened."

"Trust in him at all times, and he will deliver thy soul," responded Aunt Roxy; "God is our refuge and strength, a very present help in time of trouble. The Lord hear thee in the day of trouble; the name of the God of Jacob defend thee. Some trust in chariots and some in horses, but we will remember the name of the Lord our God. Dear Lord, hear us when we call. O my

God, I cry in the day time, but thou hearest not, and in the night season, and am not silent. Be not thou far from me. O Lord my strength, haste thee to help me."

It seemed as if those holy psalms of David, written to comfort the saints of all ages, came home with new life and sustaining power to these old Christians, as Aunt Roxy repeated them one after another.

Aunt Cily bowed her head, and when she raised it again, a gleam of comfort such as the world can neither give, nor take away, illumined her wasting, pinching features, she said more cheerfully,

"Though he slay me, yet will I trust in him."

As the hour appointed for Mr. Clay's visit approached, it required all the control which they could exert over themselves, to retain in any degree their self-possession, particularly as they were listening continually for the sound of that young foot-step, which they did not hear.

Any one to have passed the cottage or to have

dropped in, would have thought them in a very devotionally, psalm singing, happy frame of mind, for they passed from repeating the verses of the Bible to singing the fine old hymn :

"Through the love of God our Saviour,
All will be well.
Free and changeless is his favor,
All, all is well.
Precious is the blood that healed us,
Perfect is the grace that sealed us,
Strong the hand stretched out to shield us,
All must be well.

"Though we pass through tribulation,
All will be well.
Ours is such a full salvation,
All, all is well.
Happy, still in God confiding,
Fruitful, if in Christ abiding,
Holy, through the Spirit's guiding,
All must be well.

"We expect a bright to-morrow,
All will be well.
Faith can sing through days of sorrow
All, all is well.
On our Father's love relying,
Jesus every need supplying,
Or in living, or in dying,
All must be well."

This, and the hymn commencing,

> "My Jesus as thou wilt,
> Oh, may thy will be mine!"

Were great favorites with Tony's aunts to-day, and they sang them in their cracked, trembling voices, over and over again. Indeed they were very soothingly engaged in singing this last, when a knock at the door announced Mr. Clay.

Mr. Clay saw at a glance how excited and bowed the aunts were, so he came very gently in, and without attempting any other method of quieting them, than what resulted from directly meeting the cause of their excitement. He told them what arrangements he had made with regard to Tony, and then proceeded with much delicate care to rip open the stitches taken under such peculiar circumstances years ago. Taking off the handkerchief he found, as our reader already knows, the small paper covering which was Mrs. Starr's original envelope. Removing this, he came to the blue velvet bag, which had been so often, of late, described to him by her aunts, and at last he opened the stiff piece of white satin, upon which so many of the last, quickly passing hours of the mother's short life had been employed. Here was no parchment deed; all saw in a moment, that their hopes of worldly wealth were in vain; no title deeds to western lands; no money, increasing from month to month and year to year in the carefully invested funds; nothing but this piece of white satin, upon which, as Mr. Clay reverently unfolded it, he read in blue silk letters, carefully wrought, these words:

"A dying mother's legacy to her only child. May God so bless it to him, that one day it shall reunite us in heaven."

"The fear of God is the beginning of wisdom. My son, if thine heart be wise, my heart shall rejoice, even mine."

Mr. Clay read it over slowly and carefully two or three times before he put down the piece of silk, and as he did so, Aunt Cily and Roxy sat looking at him with bewildered and anxious faces.

"By God's help," he said, at last, solemnly, "this may save her boy yet. It may prove better than millions of silver or gold, it may—"

Aunt Roxy eagerly interrupted him, as she said, with quivering earnestness,

"But where shall wisdom be found? and where is the place of understanding?

"Man knoweth not the price thereof; neither is it found in the land of the living.

"The depth saith, It is not in me, and the sea saith, It is not with me.

"It cannot be gotten for gold, neither shall silver be weighed for the price thereof.

"It cannot be valued with the gold of Ophir, with the precious onyx, or the sapphire.

"The gold and the crystal cannot equal it; and the exchange of it, shall not be for jewels of fine gold.

"No mention shall be made of coral, or of pearls, for the price of wisdom is above rubies.

"The topaz of Ethiopia shall not equal it, neither shall it be valued with pure gold."

"Amen," said Aunt Cily, fervently, as she concluded, and Mr. Clay read in the holy calm and joy which overspread their time-worn faces, that God had sent them "the comforter." Not a word of repining in their secret hearts, not a feeling of regret, that the needed, almost coveted, earthly treasure had been so unexpectedly taken from them. Better than silver or jewels of fine gold, than coral or pearl, or gold of Ophir, or precious onyx, or even the radiant sapphire—this treasured hidden wisdom. It was not in the depth, it was not in the sea, and yet this mother had left it as her legacy to her son. "The fear of the Lord," repeated Aunt Cily, reverently, "the fear of the Lord."

"That is wisdom, and the very wisdom our little Tony wants," said Mr. Clay, cheerfully, "see how touchingly and beautifully his mother has enshrined in that choicest mother's blessing."

"My son, if thy heart be wise, my heart shall rejoice, even mine." Rejoicing the heart of this young dead mother; in heaven, where tears are wiped from every eye, and there shall be no more death, neither sorrow, nor crying, neither shall there be any more pain; there, even there, if this child's heart is wise, the mother's heart shall "rejoice with exceeding great joy."

The conversation which followed was long and earnest, and, as the result will be apparent in the following pages, we will not stop to detail it now.

Mr. Clay proposed, as the night was warm and cloudless, and the dew, if any, was falling, was of that soft summer kind, which drops so gently on the budding June, that Tony should be made to feel the effects of his undertaking sufficiently to be able to test its comforts if nothing more. He wished him to be allowed to wander about, as he must, and finally, very weary as he of course would be, to go to sleep upon the hard ground, supperless, tired, and with only a stone for his pillow.

The minute details of his plan he did not relate to Tony's aunts, judging, very truly, that they would suffer much more from the fear of the occurrence of an accident, than the child, should any actually take place. He knew that it was time Tony was taken from them, and put under the immediate personal care of a man; he urged this through the conversation which took place, indeed, he refused to have any thing more to do with him, unless his aunts would promise to give him up, for the next two years, entirely to him to do as he thought best. Very reluctantly the old ladies consented, with many tears and prayers and thanks, all offered in such a confused and eager way, that Mr. Clay was not sorry at a late hour to leave them to the rest which they so much needed, while he went in pursuit of the person he had sent to obtain accurate intelligence of Tony.

XI.

How Tony Ran Away.

OUR narrative must now return to Tony. On the noon of the day, when, having spent all the morning at the lime-kiln, and having been reproved by his aunt for his misconduct, he determined to do, what Nick was all the time threatening to, when any home discipline displeased him—run away. He had a very indefinite idea that there was a great deal of occupation in the world for a boy as large, and as smart as he was. That nothing would be easier than to walk to Mendon, and offer himself to the large circus company that he had ran away with Nick to see, when they were exhibiting at the neighboring town of Sodom. He had seen a boy, no larger than himself, bringing water to the horses, and then afterwards he saw him dressed up in blue velvet, covered with gold, as Tony thought, and riding that beautiful Shetland pony. Tony had envied him as he had never envied any other boy, and had managed to have a few minutes talk with "Poll," as they called him, in which he learned that it "was great fun to belong to the circus;" that he was up to his eyes in silver and gold all the time; "that both of the ponies were his, and Mr. Nixon, the manager, had promised him, when he was a little older, he would give him Fairy, the horse that danced so to music; that there was nothing equal to horses, and no boy was a boy, who did not belong to a circus and own ponies." Tony had laid all this up in his heart, and been thinking it over with much interest. If he could only get away from Mountford, his old, scolding aunts and school, and even Nick, for he was beginning to be rather tyrannical of late, how grand it would be. With these dreams, both waking and sleeping, Tony became so fully possessed, that as soon as there came a time in which he dared to utter the threat of going, he determined to put it into immediate execution; so he rose from the dinner-table, went to his room, took from his treasure drawer the articles he most valued, and was leaving the room, when his eye fell upon the small Testament which his mother had given him.

"I must have that to learn my verses in," said Tony to himself, with the strong bias of a good habit still upon him; so he put it safely away at the bottom of his pocket, and thinking only of the suit of blue velvet, in which he was hoping to ride the ponies, forgot his clothes, and went quietly out.

It was broad daylight, but Tony wished it was not so bright. It seemed to him every body he met must know precisely where he was going, and that he, Tony Starr, had actually started to run away. He almost expected the men to put their hands on his shoulder and say—

"Here, little boy, what are you about? turn around and go home."

He walked quickly by the house in which Miss Turner lived; she seemed to have such a power of finding him out, if she should see him now it would be all over. He wanted to run, but that would never do, so he put his hands into his pockets and began to walk as carelessly as he could, and to whistle just as if he was going on an errand. But, though he got bravely through one line of a negro song, his tune turned suddenly into the Methodist tune Aunt Roxy had sung him to sleep by so many—many times. Tony did not like it, so he stopped whistling, and was so still that he grew timid even before he had passed through the streets which were the most thickly inhabited. He dare not ask the road to Mendon, for fear some one would say—

"Mendon! what do you want to know that for? I guess you are running away."

So he read the sign-boards very eagerly, and

concluded which must be the right road from what he had heard Nick say. As soon as he was out of the village, and away from the houses, he felt braver, and quickened his pace. The afternoon was beautiful, so beautiful that Tony, in spite of his being such a wicked boy, and even then doing what was so wrong, felt a certain kind of happiness. The sky was very blue, the air so soft and balmy, that it seemed as if it must drop down from the sky; and then the flowers, and the grass, and the green leaves, how much they had to say. Tony could not help talking to them as he walked along, and he listened for their answers in the same way he had so many times before.

There were a whole army of birds singing, too, and Tony laughed aloud, when he thought how much of a child he must have been ever to have imagined they were God's choir—queer little things as they were. There was one peculiarity about this walk thus far, every thing Tony saw, and every thing of which he thought, seemed, by some odd chance, to bring him back to thinking of his aunts and the sitting-room, and what he had left behind him at home. He was tempted once, when he thought of his vacant seat at the table, to turn around and run back, but a second thought told him that was nothing in comparison to a seat on the pony's back, so he trudged on.

All the afternoon, it seemed to him, it grew longer and longer every half hour, instead of shortening; he walked steadily without so much as stopping to rest, but when it was really gone, and his feet and limbs began to feel tired, then he could not help thinking more and more of his aunts and the sitting-room, and the seat at the table, particularly as it was now tea time, and his long walk had made him very hungry. He wondered if he had ever heard of boys running away without having either food or money; and then he saw the clean, white shelves in the kitchen pantry, and the nice bread, and very likely, for it had been baking day, a small pie or cake made purposely for him. He found a tear or two coming into his eye, when he thought how his aunts would look and look for him, and he could not be found; and then he wondered whether they would have any other boy to whom to give the nice things, which thought made him feel very much like crying again.

Now, my readers must not for a moment suppose that Tony was sorry for what he had done, or his conscience was troubling him, very far from it, he was only hungry and tired, and, like a dog, or even an animal with no more sense than a chicken, he began to think of where he had rested and been fed, and to wish, from a natural instinct, that he was there to be fed and rested now. Still, as he was not, he plodded on his way; a little foot-sore, but not more so than he had been on many a run-away excursion with Nick.

He tried to calculate how many miles he was from Mountford, and came to the conclusion he was at least ten—half way to Mendon—for that he had heard Nick say was only twenty. Half way there and it was not dark, not more, he thought, than four o'clock in the afternoon, so, of course, eight in the evening, or nine at the farthest, would bring him to the circus. Then he would hunt out Poll, and he knew he would be very glad to see him, for he had been so friendly during the chats they had together. Perhaps he should not be too late to have a short ride on the pony before he went to bed, and if he could, how it would rest him. In spite, however, of the pleasant thought of the pony and Poll, Tony began to want his supper. He thought of the mug of milk, with the yellow cream on the top, and the white bread and butter, which was always ready for him, and he sat down to rest a minute, and try to forget them. Poll would give him a nice supper, a great deal better than he could get at home; he shouldn't be surprised if he had some broiled chicken and griddle cakes, at the thought of which favorite dishes, Tony started up, and walked on with fresh courage.

He drank from every brook he saw by the wayside, and, of course, he had to build a dam with the smooth, white stones, if the brook happened to be running pretty fast. So it began to grow dusk before he saw Mendon, or any sign-board that indicated his approach to the town. As he was looking eagerly to discover some clue to the name of the place where he now was, he saw through the twilight the friendly guide-board before him. It was just dark enough to make him remember the stories he had read of the guide boards frightening people. How some had supposed they were ghosts, standing with their great white arms, spread out to catch and devour them; and others had supposed they were highwaymen, ready to take "their money or their lives." Tony laughed heartily as he thought of these things; he felt sure such people were very timid and foolish, for he was a little boy, all alone, and there was the guide-board right before him, looking like many frightful things, if he had only a fancy for imagining them; but he had not, and was so glad to see it. He was sure he was very brave, and should soon be able to ride horses as well, and perform as many feats, as Poll himself. He ran, considering how tired he was, very nimbly to the guide-board, and then, to his surprise and dismay, he read, "Mountford, 4; Sanborn, 8; Comstock, 15; Boston, 97." No Mendon on the board. After all, then, he had mistaken his road, had walked all the afternoon, was so tired, he did not want to move another step; and what had he accomplished? four miles in the wrong direction—only four miles! foot-sore, hungry, weary as he was.

He sat down disconsolately on the green sward at the foot of the post. Small white flowers were growing there abundantly, looking up at him, with their pretty pale faces, from among the long, slender grass spears. He pulled them one by one, and made them into a small bouquet for Aunt Roxy. This was natural to him. Aunt Roxy loved flowers, and in days gone by he hardly ever saw a wild one without bringing it home to her. When he had his hand quite full, and was tying them round with a string from his pocket, he suddenly remembered that he was running away from this good, kind aunt, and might never see her again; so he dropped the flowers, and said to himself,

"But I will come back some day. When I own a pony I will ride him home, and then we will see how pleased Aunt Roxy will be, when I come prancing on his back up the garden walk."

Tony's trouble now was to know which direction to take. There was obviously nothing to be gained toward the completion of his journey by keeping on where he was. He made up his mind to knock at the door of the first house he should pass, and inquire; so as Boston was the next most desirable place to Mendon, he took the road indicated by the black finger on the board as leading to that place.

He had not walked far before he came to a small brown house, toward which he reluctantly turned. Some woman was singing her baby to sleep, and it so happened that the tune she sang was one of Aunt Cily's favorites. Encouraged by this, for it had a friendly home sound, Tony knocked gently at the door.

"Run, Maggie," said the voice, stopping the psalm; "there is some one at the door."

The door was opened by a little girl, who put a very pleasant face half way out, and in answer to Tony's question, of "How far to Mendon, and the way?" said she would ask her mother. The woman immediately came to the door with the baby in her arms, and seeing how young the child was who made the inquiries, told him to "come in, and she would talk with him about it."

This Tony was very reluctant to do; but he caught a glimpse of the tea table, neatly spread in the kitchen. It was too inviting to be resisted, and he stepped shyly in.

A great many questions were asked which he was troubled to answer. But Tony had taken sad lessons in saying what was not true lately;

so he succeeded in making what he thought a plausible story; and as the woman did not appear to doubt it, he grew bolder, and ventured to ask what he wanted so much to know. "Mendon was in quite another direction. He must pass through Mountford, leaving the town in an opposite direction from the one which he had taken, if he wished to reach it. It was a hard road, up hill and down, pretty slow travelling for a horse, and a great deal worse for a foot-passenger."

Tony was troubled. To go back through Mountford was impossible. No; ninety-seven miles and Boston at last was a great deal better; so, as that was some distance, he felt he must not stop, and was hurrying away, when the woman called him back to give him a couple of crackers and a large ginger cake.

"I don't know who you are," she said, kindly, "and my heart misgives me, little boy, that you are doing something which is wrong. If you have run away, I hope you will go straight home, for your folks will be anxious about you after it gets to be dark. Be a good child, and go back; they won't do anything to you if you tell the truth about it."

Tony went away quickly, not forgetting to thank her for his supper, but afraid she would insist on his going home, which he was not yet prepared to do. He sat down under the guide-board once more, to eat his crackers,—his cake he had determined to store away until the next morning for his breakfast, for as he meant to walk on through the night, he had no doubt he should be very hungry then.

He felt quite refreshed with the rest, and the crackers, and the sound of the home hymn; so he started bravely again, but found, after a short distance, that it was very hard work to put one foot before the other. He wished he could creep up into his small room, with its neat, white-covered bed, and the pictures hung on the blue walls, and go to sleep. He must rest again so soon, and he was a long, long way off from Boston. He wished he could go into a barn, as he had read of so many runaway boys doing, and sleep on a large hay mow. Next to his own little room, this seemed the pleasantest place in the world; but there was no building of any kind within sight, not even a tree for a roof. He climbed up on the stone wall to look about him. At a little distance was a clump of barberry bushes; if he could get in behind these, he would be safe from observation and could take a nap: then when he woke up, rested and refreshed, he would start again, and before daylight he should be a long distance toward his future home.

Tony did not know much of the nature of barberry bushes; so he got many deep scratches as he pushed and pulled his way in under them. But at last there he was, in as nice a place as if he had built it on purpose. The branches of the bush grew very closely together, and were covered with a small green leaf, which made a thick curtain around him.

Beside these there were plenty of hanging yellow blossoms, very delicate, and with a soft perfume which was quite agreeable. Tony thought as he saw them indistinctly in the deepening twilight, that, hanging against the leaves as they did, they looked like some pretty flowers painted on his green window shades; then he almost fancied, as the evening breeze moved them gently hither and thither, that they were little fairies come to nestle with him in this pretty green bower, and so, without any further troubled thoughts of home, or his aunts, he fell asleep.

Toward midnight, however, he awoke. He moved about uneasily on his hard bed, and in every one of these half-asleep, careless motions he came so sharply in contact with the thorns that very soon he was wide awake, and in a great deal of pain.

It was a long time, and not until he had several quite severe injuries, that the consciousness of where he was came fully to him. He could not see the sky, as he had on the night when he had fallen asleep in the woods, after being left by Nick and Lot; and if he could have, the pure, good stars were never lit up in the heavens to be any comfort or company to a child who was running away. It seemed to Tony very dark, very cold, very uncomfortable, and he the most miserable boy that ever lived. Now indeed, he wished most sincerely he had never run away; now, indeed, neither Poll nor the pony had any charms for him, if he only could be at home with his dear old aunts again.

Tony began to think for the first time for many months, of his prayers; and a feeling that he was not good enough to pray,—that God would not listen to such a bad boy—came over him with a force which it never had before. He felt more frightened and alone than ever; and covering his face with both of his hands, he moaned in a very heart-breaking manner.

If he could only ask God to take care of him through the long, dark hours, and to forgive him for what he had done wrong, and to let him live to see the light of another morning, so that he could go home, how thankful he should be.

Tony never thought, he was but a child, of how much his aunts must be suffering; if he had he would have been even more unhappy. But now he thought only of himself, and how wicked a boy he was. It seemed to him, as he lay there, as if every falsehood he had told, and every wicked word he had said, came up before him. God sent the memory to make him see and feel how wicked he had been.

Tony closed his eyes very tightly, and tried to shut out the leaves around him; but it was of no use, he could not keep them so, they would open. And then it seemed to him his sorrow and repentance grew greater and greater, as the night grew darker and colder.

The thorns, too, on the bushes, how merciless they were! A motion to rid himself of them on one side, always brought him into closer contact with them on the other. At last it was not to be borne any longer; and Tony, the most miserable of boys, crept out from under the bush, and sat crouching, shivering, and frightened, under the stars and the still night sky.

"If I could only ask God to take care of me," again sobbed Tony; "but he is so angry with the wicked every day." And then, by some strange association, and as if to show him how very lonely, and desolate, and sinful he was, this beautiful hymn, which Tony loved so much and used to sing at home every Sabbath night, came into his mind; and, sitting there, he repeated it aloud very slowly and distinctly,—the little ripples of the night air standing still to listen to it as he did so.

"Around the throne of God in heaven,
Thousands of children stand,—
Children, whose sins are all forgiven,
A holy, happy band.

"What brought them to that world above,
That heaven so bright and fair?
Where all is peace, and joy, and love,
How came those children there?

"Because the Saviour shed his blood
To wash away their sin;
Bathed in that pure and precious flood,
Behold them white and clean.

"On earth they sought their Saviour's grace,
On earth they loved his name;
So now they see his blessed face,
And stand before the Lamb."

Tony had an indistinct idea that at some other time there had been children who had done wrong as he had, but who had been "washed in their Saviour's blood," and now, "white and clean," were standing all together, "thousands" of them, "before the throne of God in heaven." Tony thought they must be a very "happy band," and that it would be far preferable to be there, with them, than to be sitting here all alone, and so wicked on earth, and then he thought if he came to Jesus, and told him how guilty he was, and how he meant to go home the next morning, and never say a wicked word, or do what was wrong any more, that perhaps there would be some of the blood remaining in which Jesus would wash him, and forgive him, and help him to be a better boy in the future.

Tony was thinking all this very busily over, when he heard the sound of wheels coming in the direction of the place where he was sitting. His first thought was to secrete himself, for fear it should be some one who would do him injury; but again he thought he should escape notice perhaps better by keeping still, than he should if he tried to run and hide, so he sat very motionless, though his heart beat so loud he could almost hear it.

Very soon a chaise, drawn by a white horse, came near. Tony could see the horse, though it was pretty dark, and it reminded him at once of Mr. Clay's. Oh if it should be he, and he would take him in, and carry him home, what a different boy he would be for his whole future life.

As the chaise came opposite him, it stopped. Tony seemed almost to expect it, and it did not surprise him much to hear Mr. Clay say,

"Tony, is that you?"

"Yes, sir," said Tony.

"Should you like to get in and ride home with me?"

"Yes, sir."

"Very well, give me hold of your hand; spring quickly, Kate don't like to stand in the dark."

Tony held up his cold, trembling hands very eagerly, but could not "spring quickly," he was too tired and stiff for that, so Mr. Clay lifted him into the chaise, wrapped him warmly in a shawl he had brought for that purpose, and turned the horse's head in the direction of Mountford.

Not a word did either of them speak. Tony, after a little subdued crying, fell back in the chaise, and pretty soon his head dropped over heavily on Mr. Clay's arm.

"Poor boy," he said, laying it down gently on his lap, "this is a hard experience for such a child; but, who can doubt that it is God sent?"

The next thing Tony knew, he was laid upon a sofa, and when he waked late on the following day, he recognized, after some trouble, the objects round him to be those belonging to Mr. Clay's office. It may well be imagined that all his ideas at first were confused and indistinct, but by degrees they returned clearly to him, and he lifted his head to look into an adjoining room, and see Mr. Clay busily writing at his table.

Mr. Clay raised his eyes for a moment, and Tony saw he knew that he was awake, but he did not move or speak to him.

XII.

Tony Receives the Legacy.

MR. CLAY continued his writing, it seemed to Tony, a long, long time. At last it was finished, Tony watched him put the papers all neatly away, without daring to move.

He almost began to hope Mr. Clay had forgotten him, and when he went home to dinner, he could run quietly back to his aunts. I am sorry to say, that many of Tony's good resolutions, made in the dark and fright of the night before, faded away when he found himself safe and well in Mountford. He began to think what he could say to his aunts, that would excuse his running away, and had nearly decided to say he went out for a walk, and lost his way, so he could not get home, when Mr. Clay came into his room and put down by him, still without speaking, a glass of water, and two slices of dry bread, then turned and left the office, locking the door after him, and taking the key. Tony did not dare to call, indeed Mr. Clay looked so stern and cold that he could not speak even if he had tried, and so Tony pushed away his bread and water, laid down again, and began to think.

He was a prisoner, with prisoner's fare, bread and water. Not many months ago Mr. Clay had told him if he was not a better boy he must go to the House of Correction, where they sent the worst children; he wondered now if it was not Mr. Clay's intention to send him there, and this was breaking him into it, showing him what kind of a life it was to be. Tony of course began to feel alarmed, he almost wished he had hidden himself so that Mr. Clay could not have found him; but he would get up and move around the office while he was away, any thing was better than staying where he was another minute, with that clock ticking, ticking so without a pause, it became almost like a hand that touched him each time it ticked; he thought that if Mr. Clay had given him a scolding it would be so much pleasanter than his silence and this clock.

By-and-by Tony began to listen for Mr. Clay's return, he intended to go back and lie down on the sofa as if he had not moved from there during his absence, and he had many false alarms, other feet came up the stairs, but they turned into other rooms, and Tony saw the longest afternoon of his life drag wearily by, without Mr. Clay's return. It began to grow a little dusk, and Tony, more and more alarmed at the uncertainty of every thing. Now, if Mr. Clay would only come; he forgot his plan of deceiving him by going again to the sofa; he forgot all the stories by which he had meant to excuse his absence to his aunts. He had only one thought, how soon would Mr. Clay come. About five hours after he went out, Mr. Clay unlocked the door and entered. Tony was sitting in a chair in the middle of the room, the very image of distress and repentance. Mr. Clay felt his heart soften toward the child the moment his eye fell upon him. He was pale, and looked so unlike the happy, laughing, noisy Tony Starr, that Mr. Clay repeated to himself almost involuntarily the verse, "The way of transgressors is hard."

"Tony," he said, gently, "Do you know this is your tenth birth-day?"

Tony started; in his misery and sin he had entirely forgotten it; and this was surprising, because his aunts had attached so much importance to it, they had given him a vague idea that it was to be the greatest day of his life.

"No, sir," said Tony, without daring to look up.

"Yes, it is; put on your cap and come with me; or stop, Mrs. Clay has sent your supper, you may eat that first. Are you hungry?"

"No, sir;" and Tony's voice trembled, but when he saw the nice-looking bread and cake which Mr. Clay unrolled from a bundle he had laid upon the table, he said quickly,

"Yes, sir, I believe I am."

"Very well, eat."

Tony obeyed, thinking of nothing else but how good it tasted, as the food quickly disappeared.

"Now come, are you ready?"

Tony put on his cap and moved toward the door.

"Stop, it is locked;" and the sound of the key, as it turned in the lock, Tony never forgot.

When they were once more in the familiar street, Tony felt an almost irresistible inclination to run home as fast as he could, but he dared not; he glanced up at Mr. Clay, he looked more kindly than he had in the morning, perhaps he was taking him to the House of Correction, and felt sorry for him, he wished he would tell him if he was, he should like to be prepared for it.

But Mr. Clay did not seem inclined to talk, he walked quickly to the part of the town which led away, Tony saw, from his aunts' house. Where could he be going? he knew there was no House of Correction there; perhaps a wagon was waiting to carry him, and he should never see his aunts any more. Tony felt some large tears roll down his cheeks as he thought of this, but he wiped them quickly away with the back of his hand, he did not like Mr. Clay to see them.

Very soon they turned off from the main road into the one leading to the cemetery. Tony had gone with his aunts over it many times, when they were taking him, to carry fresh flowers to his mother's grave. He stopped now, and picked a little bunch of violets, which grew by the wayside.

"What are those for, Tony?" asked Mr. Clay. These were the first words he had spoken for a long time.

"For my mother's grave," said Tony, hesitatingly. "If you would just stop a moment and let me run in and put them there; Aunt Cily says she loved flowers dearly, and I should like so much to leave them there before I go."

Mr. Clay was touched, the boy had something good left in him still.

"We are going there, Tony," he said. "You shall leave them, if you like."

Very reverently Mr. Clay opened the small gate which led them into the consecrated ground. He looked so solemn and sad, that Tony could not help wondering if he had some one he loved sleeping in all the green mounds they passed.

Tony's mother was buried in a remote corner of the cemetery. The aunts had taken much care of the spot. They had placed a weeping-willow at the head of the plain, white slab, and around the grave some of the roses that they loved so well in their own trim garden. Indeed, there was hardly a grave in the humble burying-ground, that showed so much persevering care and attention; for they had thought not only of the dead, but of the living, wishing to link the memory of that mother with her young child's life, so that it might be an ever-present, active influence.

"It is the prettiest grave in Mountford," said Tony, as they came in sight of it. "See, Mr. Clay, there is not another one with so many roses. Here are white and red, and my moss rose has a large bud springing from it,"—turning the beautiful bud toward Mr. Clay—" Aunt Roxy said it would live and flourish if I was a good boy."

"And have you been, Tony?" asked Mr. Clay.

"No, sir!—No, sir! I thought it would die. I remembered it many times when I was going to do what was wrong, and didn't do it, for fear it would. But it hasn't, you see, sir; here it is."

"Ah Tony, Tony! God is better to you than you deserve. Now listen to me."

And then and there, Mr. Clay told Tony the whole story of the Legacy, of his young, sainted mother, of her prayers and tears and efforts for him, and finally read to him the words which she had wrought for him nine years ago.

Tony listened to him, with tears dropping from his eyes upon the grave; and when Mr. Clay put into his trembling hands the small, blue, velvet bag, and bade him unfold and read for himself, the carefully-shaped letters wavered to and fro, and mechanically he repeated what he could not see to read.

"May God help you, Tony Starr," said Mr. Clay, solemnly. "Kneel, and ask him for his forgiveness and his blessing."

The setting sun cast upon the grave the shadow of a little form with folded hands; and over the mouldering heart of the dead mother passed, it may be, one throb of that joy which she had promised to her son, if his "heart was wise."

Poor Tony! That wisdom for him is still among the hidden things. But it is in the hands of that covenant-keeping God, who "understandeth the way thereof, and he knoweth the place thereof;" who hath said that he will hear the prayer of the righteous, and his ears shall be open unto their cry.

XIII.

Poll the Circus Boy.

TONY passed the night of his tenth birth-day, once more, and for the last time for many coming months, in his small attic room; Aunt Cily came up to weep and pray over him, and Aunt Roxy joined in the prayers and the tears, as the sound of them came down to her in the room below. Close by his bed stood the trunk his mother had brought with her when she came to the house; it was packed and strapped all ready for an early morning start. And just at daylight, Mr. Clay, with the chaise and the white horse, stopped at the door.

All the family had been up for some time. Tony had had the nicest of breakfasts, with every favorite dish his indulgent aunts could command. He sat now, as Mr. Clay came, with his cap on, ready to open the door; and before Mr. Clay had time to get out, he was at his side.

"I am all ready, sir," he said. "The trunk is not heavy; I brought it down myself from up stairs. I can put it in the rack without your moving."

Mr. Clay watched him bring it out, saw that he put it carefully on and drew the large strap tightly; then, after running in to kiss his aunts good-bye, Tony climbed into the chaise, and without looking back, or trusting himself to speak, sat closely up into the corner, and Mr. Clay was sure he heard a suppressed sob.

For some time they rode on quietly. This was an hour Mr. Clay wished the boy to remember as long as he lived; therefore, he took no pains to divert him until the sun was high in the heavens, and the earth and sky were full of those beautiful, inviting things which God sends to make us happy. Then Mr. Clay began to talk with Tony, and the boy grew gradually interested in what he said, so that before they had passed over many miles, Tony, in spite of the occasion of his ride, felt happy.

About three o'clock they came to a place which Tony looked eagerly to see, for Mr. Clay told him it was Mendon. Very soon after they entered the town they heard the music of a band, and Mr. Clay said, "Here is the circus, I presume, by the music. I hope it will not be near the tavern where I must stop, for there is apt to be a great deal of confusion and wickedness around, wherever it is."

Tony hung his head. What would Mr. Clay have said, if he had known he left home with the intention of joining this very circus? As they drove up to the Mendon House, where Mr. Clay felt it necessary to bait his horse, Tony saw that the yard was full of men and horses, and the piazza crowded with such a rabble as he had never seen together before.

If the next stopping-place had not been twelve miles distant, Mr. Clay would have driven on, rather than to have encountered such a motley crowd. But the day's journey was long, so that it would not do to overtask the horse at the outset, particularly as he must be driven back on the following day. There was no help; so driving through as well as he could, Mr. Clay succeeded in getting attention only because he was personally known to the landlord, and his character and station everywhere commanded respect.

There was no private room, however, to be had; and after a little while, Mr. Clay having private business to transact in town, was obliged to leave Tony to take care of himself, while he went out.

At first Tony sat very still, and felt frightened at being alone where there was so much confusion and wickedness; but by degrees, when he saw no one took any notice of him, he grew more courageous, and soon he began to think of Poll, and to wonder where he was, and if he could not find him. So he left the place where Mr. Clay had advised him to stay, and stole out to the stable the back way. As he passed a small corn barn, a little separated from the main building, he heard the sound of a heavy whip descending rapidly, followed by shrieks and cries for mercy so heart-rending, that he stopped as if chained to the spot. As he did so, he heard distinctly,

"Oh, don't! don't! I never will fall off again. Mercy! mercy!"

"You did it on purpose, you know you did. There,—take that, and that, and that, and see if you can't mind your business better next time. I'll teach you to drop off and let him run."

"I was so tired; I never will again. Oh! oh! oh!"

The blows ceased, and Tony finding all was still, crept up to the barn, and looked through one of the large chinks. On a heap of old straw in the corner of the building lay a boy, no larger, Tony thought, than he was himself, wringing his hands and weeping bitterly. Tony thought he looked like Poll, but as his back was turned to him, he could not see distinctly. A man was hanging up a horsewhip which he had evidently been using; he was very red in the face, and while he was hanging it he continued to abuse the boy in language which I should be very sorry to repeat.

"You will stay here," he said, as he turned to go out, "until dark; then if you make another blunder to-night, I won't leave a whole bone in your body."

"May I have something to eat?" asked the boy.

"No!" said the man, gruffly. "Digest your horsewhipping; that is all you'll get to-day."

Then he slammed the door after him, and went out. And when the boy was sure he was gone, he began to groan, and cry, and wring his hands as if his very heart was broken. As he turned toward the crack, Tony saw he was not mistaken. It was, indeed, the much-envied Poll, but how changed! Out from his showy trappings, in his old, torn, soiled dress, Tony saw only a puny, pale lad, with his eyes very red, his cheek swollen from the blow which had been inflicted upon it, and his lip bleeding from another sharp cut. For a few minutes Poll continued to cry, and moan, and Tony to watch him. At last he laid down upon the straw, and Tony saw that his hands unclasped and fell down at his side; so he supposed he must have fallen asleep. Creeping back into the house, Tony found Mr. Clay had not returned; and while he sat there, anxiously watching for him, the red-faced man came into the room, and began to talk very loudly and coarsely of his ponies, and the wonders they could perform.

"You have got a nice little chap to ride them," said one of the bystanders, "if he did fall off last night. How that black pony flew round! I thought in my heart he would knock some of the children down before you could catch him."

"He a'n't used to mistakes, you see," said the man, with an ugly wink: "but the chap he got left by some blunder, and had to foot it ten mile, so he was kind of tired, and couldn't set him quite as firm as usual. But there a'n't a smarter boy nor pony to be found in these 'ere United States of Ameriky than them two. They make a pair, I tell you; I make more money by 'um than by all the other horse-flesh I own."

"Do you call the boy horse-flesh?" asked another man laughing.

"Why yes; its all one, you know; the pony a'n't nothing without the boy, nor the boy a'n't nothing without the pony, so I take it, they mean pretty much the same thing."

"He's as pretty a little fellow as there is out," said a woman, who had edged her way up close to the speaker.

"Which, marm," asked the man, "the boy or the pony?"

"Why, both on 'um; but the boy I meant.

"He's well enough, but he a'n't, as I said, nothing alone; them's one."

"And you treat the pony better than the boy," said another.

"Well, yes, I kind of guess I do, 'cause there

a'n't no more ponies to be had, and as for the boys, bless me, if they don't plague me nigh to death ; I never go nowhere, that there a'n't some fifty after me, to git Poll's place. I have to take my horse-whip to them sometimes, jist to git rid of 'um."

"And to this one, too? I should think from the screaming I heard just now," said the same man.

"Well—yes ; I have to give him Jarsif now and then, or he would be getting tired and tumbling off all the time ; boys and horses flourish better for a good smart blow now and then, it kind of brings their senses to a pint, you know."

Many of the crowd were mean and wicked enough to laugh when they heard what this man meant for a joke ; but Tony trembled all over, and when he remembered how he had wished to be under his power, he felt almost afraid the man would know it, too, and claim him. It seemed a very long time to Tony while Mr. Clay was away. He was glad when he told him he was to go, for he thought he should be at liberty to run about among the horses and men, and do what he pleased; but he had felt no inclination, after he saw Poll, to venture outside the door; he stationed himself at the window and waited eagerly for Mr. Clay's coming, and when he saw him, ran out to meet him, with so troubled a face that Mr. Clay immediately asked:

"Tony, what is the matter?"

"Oh, Mr. Clay!" said Tony, speaking so quickly that his words could hardly find vent. "They have got Poll in that barn, and the man whips him with a great big horse-whip, until he is all swollen and bloody, and then he says he wont give him any thing to eat, and he must ride the pony again to-night, and if he falls off, he will break every bone in his body. Oh, Mr. Clay, do, do!"

"Who is Poll? and what can I do?" asked Mr. Clay.

"He is the boy that rides the ponies."

"How do you know?"

Tony hesitated for a moment, then looking Mr. Clay firmly in the face, and recalling his good resolutions, made on the previous night, he said,

"I know, because Nick and I ran away from school, when the circus was at Sodom, and went to it, and I saw and talked with Poll a great deal, when Nick didn't know it. He told me so many famous stories, that I—I—" Tony hesitated, but after a moment went bravely on, "I thought he must be the happiest boy in the world, and when I ran away day before yesterday, I meant to come to Mendon and join him."

Tony looked as if he thought Mr. Clay would catch him up and repeat the whipping Poll had had, on the spot; but to his surprise, Mr. Clay only smiled and held out his hand.

"That is a good, brave boy, Tony," he said, "come, we will go and see to Poll, if that is his name. Where is he?"

"Out in the corn barn;" and Tony, still holding Mr. Clay's hand, led him toward the barn.

"Stop, Tony," said Mr. Clay, just before they reached it, "I had better see the man who has the care of this boy first; perhaps he has done something very wrong, and deserved this whipping."

Tony repeated all he had heard the man say to Poll, and in the tavern; and Mr. Clay, believing him, went again toward the barn.

To Tony's surprise, instead of peeping through the chinks as he had, he opened the door and went in, Tony timidly following him. There lay Poll asleep on the bundle of straw, but moaning still, as if in pain. His hand was under his swollen cheek, and his lip had become so discolored from the blood, which had coagulated upon it, that it made a very distressed being to look upon; Mr. Clay stooped tenderly over him.

"Poor little fellow," he said, "he is most shamefully injured, whatever the cause may have been. Do you know the man who struck him?"

"Yes, sir; I should know him among a thousand," whispered Tony; "but do waken Poll,

Mr. Clay, and give him something to eat, I know he is very hungry."

"Not yet; come and show me the man."

Tony easily recognized him; and Mr. Clay approaching him, and touching him on the shoulder, said, "A word with you if you please." The man stared roughly in his face; but there was something about Mr. Clay which demanded instant respect and attention; so he followed him out from among the crowd, to a spot by themselves, where Tony saw them walking up and down as if they were engaged in an earnest, and, on the circus man's part, angry conversation.

When Mr. Clay returned he looked very soberly, and Tony heard him order his horse, with a feeling of dismay. Could it be that he would go away and leave Poll. Tony could hardly believe it; but then no order was given for his release, and Tony, at last too excited to wait patiently any longer, came to Mr. Clay and said:

"May I just go and give him this little bundle of cakes, Aunt Roxy put up for me? I know a hole close by where he was asleep, plenty large enough to put it through."

"You may do any thing you can for him, Tony," said Mr. Clay, kindly. "The man who has the care of him, has him legally bound to him, so that I can do nothing to help him, without going through a long course of law, though I have threatened him with instant punishment if he is so brutal to him again; that is all I can do now; you may help him all you are able to, and—here, Mr. Smith," calling the landlord, "let me have some substantial slices of bread and butter and cold meat;—those will be better for him, Tony, than your aunt's cakes, nice as they are."

When the bread and meat was brought, Tony wrapped them carefully up in paper, and taking much pains to keep out of the red faced man's sight, he went once more to the corn barn.

Coming unobserved to the large hole he had

before noticed, he looked through it, and saw Poll was awake, and was sitting up, but looking even paler and thinner than he did when he was asleep. Tony whispered very softly,

"Poll! Poll!"

"Who wants me?" said the boy, starting and looking in a frightened way about him.

"Its no one but me—Tony Starr," said Tony; "I have brought you some nice dinner, Mr. Clay bought for you. Here I am; don't you see me in this big hole?" and Tony thrust his arm and the food through. The boy sprang at them like a famished dog, and without any thanks, or even looking to see who had brought it to him, devoured slice after slice, in a manner which astonished Tony.

"Here are my cakes, Aunt Roxy gave me; they are very nice," he whispered, as he saw Poll stop to take breath.

"Who are you?" said the boy, now able to think of something beside food.

"My name is Tony Starr. Don't you know I

saw you and talked with you ever so long when you were at Sodom?"

"No, I don't remember you; but how came you to find me out here?"

"I listened, and I heard *him* whip you."

"Did you?" and Poll's face grew very red.

"Yes; I thought it was too bad, and I told Mr. Clay, so I guess he won't dare to do it any more."

"He always does; he'll kill me yet," said Poll, "and I wish he would, I had rather die than live so."

"Don't be afraid, I guess he won't again. What made you fall off the pony?"

"I was so tired I couldn't sit him; I hadn't had any supper either, and things went round dizzy like."

"Don't you want to run away?"

"I have, ever so many times, but he always catches and brings me back, and then he flogs me so I can but just move; once he thought he had broken my back, and I thought so too, and that I should die, but I didn't, you see," said Poll, disconsolately.

At this moment Tony heard some one opening the barn door, he moved away from the hole, and Poll secreted what was left of his food quickly under the straw. It was the circus master, who evidently afraid of some interference on Mr. Clay's part, had come to see that all was safe. He started when he saw how Poll's face looked, and swore at him some very terrible oaths, as if he was the cause of his own disfigurement.

Tony was very much frightened, and ran back to the tavern to tell Mr. Clay, he was afraid Poll was going to be whipped again; but Mr. Clay had already spoken to two or three men, who were to watch and interfere in any such emergency; so as his horse was rested and ready, he took Tony once more with him, and they renewed their journey, both of them with many troubled thoughts of Poll. Toward night they reached the place of their destination, a small pleasant village, situated like Mountford, among the mountains. Here, they drove directly to Tony's new home, the house of the minister. This clergyman was a brother of Mrs. Clay's, and one to whose care, Mr. Clay, after much thought, had decided to entrust Tony, for the present. In so doing, he had consulted the boy's best good. To remove him for a time from the too indulgent care of his aunts, and from the bad associates in whom he had become interested, in Mountford, to give him an entire change of scene and influences, Mr. Clay thought might be the most reliable way of strengthening those good promises and resolutions which Tony had recently made under such solemn circumstances. Mr. Clay thought very justly, that nothing can be more hardening to a child than to bring just such influences to bear upon him, if they do not result in an immediate and sensible good, he had therefore written all the facts of Tony's life to this good brother-in-law, and as he had a large family of well-behaved children of his own, had easily persuaded him to open his heart and home, to one more, one of God's children, for such, in a literal sense, he considered the orphans of pious parents to be.

Mr. Fuller was eminently qualified for just such a trust, and his wife was a willing and able helpmate ; they received Tony as if he were a lost child coming home, and the boy nestling down among the other children, with senses all on the alert, and a touched, susceptible heart, saw Mr. Clay return to Mountford with hardly a wish to accompany him, only whispering to him as he left,

" Mr. Clay, please, sir, don't forget Poll ; and give my love to my aunts, and Alice."

So began a new era in Tony's life, through which the already-prolonged pages of our book will not allow us to follow him ; we must pass over the next two years, and present him to our readers at the expiration of that time, a grown and altered boy. A boy to whom had been fulfilled those covenant promises, so sacred and holy, so full of trust and hope to the believer, whose eye, closing for ever upon earthly scenes, sees with keen vision into the secret place of the Most High ; and, it may be, is allowed to read there, that not one jot or tittle of those promises shall in any wise pass away, until all be fulfilled.

XIV.

Tony's New Life.

DURING these last two years Tony had made several visits to his old aunts, but had never been allowed to remain but a few days at a time. He was now to go home to live once more, and he heard the announcement with a strange mingling of joy and sorrow.

He had become very much attached to his new home, to Mr. and Mrs. Fuller, and the adopted brothers and sisters; but, after all, there was a natural feeling that they were not his own, and at times, a longing for the home close by the side of the Methodist meeting-house.

We said in our last chapter, that in Tony Starr had been fulfilled those covenant promises made so long ago to the holy parents of old.

Mr. and Mrs. Fuller had been freely informed by Mr. Clay of all the circumstances attending the making of Tony's Legacy by his dead mother, and the delivery of it to him, at the time which she had appointed. This, with much care and judgment, they often brought before the mind of the child, presenting, perhaps, two courses of conduct to him, and asking him which seemed most truly "wise," or urging him to a duty, because it implied the "fear of God."

We cannot pause to enter into details; we would simply say, that God, in his infinite mercy and love, moved the heart of this child, through the instrumentality of this precious Legacy, to seek a close union with himself. Humbled, in view of his past sins, bitterly mourning over them, he sought forgiveness through the blood of Christ. There shall be joy in heaven over one sinner that repenteth; the heart of Tony's mother, among that heavenly host, "shall rejoice;" and may we not believe that the Holy Spirit, under whose direct influences Tony's stubborn heart melted, may have whispered to him in these words of joy, which were mingling in the mother's "glad new song."

Tony's conversion was a marked and radical change. It showed itself, as it always must, in the little details of his every-day life; but, poor child! he had still so many sins to mourn, so many weaknesses to pray over, so many falling steps to retrace, still we may hope that he has found that fear of the Lord, "which is the beginning of wisdom."

Prayer evidently, in Tony's case, had been the cause of his conversion—prayers of the dead ancestors—prayers of the young, lost mother—prayers of the maiden aunts.

Ah, yes! there are none of us who will faint and grow weary by the way, if we may be spared this one inestimable privilege. If we may bring to our Father in heaven, not only our wants spiritual and temporal of the passing day, but if we may lay also into those everlasting arms the whole burden of our hearts' weary load, when we think of the future for those we love, dependent now upon our constant watchfulness and care, if we may leave it there, faint and heavy laden, though we be, surely we shall find rest. Under the wing of this angel, Tony's mother fell asleep, and though it has been folded and drooping since, for the sin stain the boy's life has cast upon it, yet now it is spread once again, and slowly, very slowly, is taking its flight back to the side of that ancient mercy seat.

There were circumstances, too, in the home circle which made it almost necessary for Tony to return; Aunt Cily, for the past year, had been growing more and more feeble. She seemed to have no disease, nothing to which the physicians could give a name, and yet it was very evident that, month by month, she was failing. At first it showed itself only in growing easily weary. The nice work Aunt Roxy must do, and then, almost before they knew, or were prepared for it, she found she could not sew at all; but could only busy herself over the house work. Then came a time when even that grew too arduous for her, and then Aunt Roxy began to wait upon her, first only in slight, hardly conscious ways; but, before Tony came home, dress-making was again almost given up at the cottage, and the sofa, which had been bought for the solace of his mother's last days, was rolled into the sitting-room, and when Tony returned, he found Aunt Cily on it, looking even paler and thinner than ever, and supported by pillows. But Tony had come back, he was their own again; and in the joy of this, for the first week after his arrival, Aunt Cily seemed to recover rapidly. The doctor said the "change was wonderful, that a merry heart did more good than medicine; that Tony was the best little nurse in Mountford," and many other things, which made the boy feel proud and happy. He was now twelve years old, and a fine, stout-looking child; indeed, there was something so manly, such a childish dignity about him, that it created in the simple hearts of his old aunts a kind of wonder, half akin to awe.

Could this be the same boy that they had carried in their arms, trotted on their knees, and to whom they had sung lullabies? Tony had the same loving look in his eyes, that he had then, and with this he answered them, when their doubts grew strong. Now, he was, as they said, "so handy and so thoughtful," Aunt Cily did not seem to have a wish but he knew it before she did, or, at least, so she fancied, and it was a very pleasant fancy. He brought her cold water every time that in her tumbler was becoming warm; he put the footstool in precisely the right place, at the right moment; he fixed her pillows so nicely; and best, and, most dearly prized of all, he was willing to read to her, as long as she was able to listen, that precious Bible, which grew every day more and more precious, as she went tottering down into the dark valley.

What a comfort he was, and how fervently

with prayers, and glad songs of grateful joy; the aunts thanked the Giver of all Good for this restored child.

Aunt Roxy also found Tony of great use. He was so much company, saved her so many steps; was always so cheerful, and ready to run on any errand, and was such a protection! for these last years were years of so much feebleness and anxiety, that the natural yearning for some one to lean upon had grown strong, and difficult to bear in the hearts of the lonely maiden aunts. Tony was, to be sure, only a child, but he was theirs; and he showed so much judgment and such a capacity for care-taking, that they must be forgiven if he had been but a short time at home before they allowed cares to devolve upon him which were very unusual for one of his years.

Through the summer Aunt Cily lingered; but, after the first excitement of Tony's coming home, gradually grew less and less able to sit up, and when the chill autumn winds began to blow, then she called Tony to her, and blessed him. Blessed him with the old patriarchal blessing; blessed him in the name of the covenant-keeping God, and thus adding one more link to the strength of these solemn promises, fell asleep, while her sister and Tony were singing her favorite hymn—

"Rock of ages, cleft for me."

Closed her weary, time-worn eyes here, to open them in that other better world, where age and sickness, and death may never come, and then Aunt Roxy knew that she was left alone, with no one to love or to be loved by, but the orphan nephew; and Tony, as he stood by the lifeless form of his aunt, repeated slowly and solemnly her last blessing, linking it in some mysterious way with the Legacy, and the inheritance of that true wisdom, which his mother had asked for him.

Four weeks after they had laid Aunt Cily by his mother's side, Tony knocked softly at Mr.

Clay's office door for admission. The gentleman was in, and quite willing, as usual, to listen to the request which he knew Tony had come to bring.

In some measure he looked upon the boy as belonging to him. God had made him one of the means of restoring him from what had seemed to him an almost hopeless state of wickedness; hopeless if it had not been for the covenant promises, and what was only the same thing in another form, the bringing those promises forcibly to mind in the mother's legacy. Mr. Clay was well convinced that the change in Tony was radical, that with the usual tenacity of purpose which had always been so marked a characteristic, having once made up his mind to seek after the true wisdom, he was not going to rest satisfied with any counterfeits. Every good resolution had been strengthened by the life and influences of the last two years, and now, when he saw it was Tony who had knocked, and saw the earnest expression of face with which he entered, he had granted the request before it was made.

"I have come, Mr. Clay," said Tony, "to tell you Mr. Hurlburt has asked me to come as clerk into his book-store. May I go, sir?"

"What inducements does he offer you?"

"One hundred dollars a year, if I board at home, sir. Only think of it, one hundred dollars, won't that make Aunt Roxy rich?"

"It will certainly be quite a help, but in the mean time, what is to become of the education you have commenced? Here is a letter from Mr. Fuller, in which he urges me to see that you keep on with your studies. He says you do very finely in the classics."

Tony's eyes shone with delight. "Thank you, sir," he said, "and thank Mr. Fuller too. I do love my Latin above every thing, but you see, sir, that will not buy clothes or food for us now, and I should be very much grieved to see Aunt Roxy wanting either while she has such a great, stout boy to work and get them for her."

"But the education, Tony, the education. If you should lose two or three years now, you will probably be obliged to give it up altogether."

"I should be very sorry, sir," and Tony held his head down, and blushed deeply; "but I don't see any other way at present. If God means me to be educated, he will show me how I can be so at some future time. Now, if you please, I should like to go to Mr. Hurlburt."

"You see clearly what you are doing Tony, so that at some future day you will not say with regret, 'Why did Mr. Clay allow me?' You remember, too, that your father was a professional man, and that you have an almost inherited right to an education if you wish it."

"I know it all, sir. I have thought it over and over a great many times since I came home, and my conclusion is, if you are willing, to do my duty in the present, and let the future alone, God will take care of it."

"You have my full consent, Tony;" and Mr. Clay's voice had a very cordial tone, which Tony loved to hear. "How soon must you go?"

"This afternoon, he said, sir."

"So soon! well, if it is to be done, the sooner the better. What does Aunt Roxy say?"

"I have not told her yet, sir; I thought I would ask you first, but now, I will run directly home, and she shall consent in five minutes."

Mr. Clay smiled, and Tony quickly disappeared.

That noon Tony went to his new occupation of clerk in Mr. Hurlburt's book-store, and Aunt Roxy, taking her seat by the window from which she could catch the first view of him on his return, watched and sewed, and sang psalms and gave thanks until his return.

Tony threw himself with much ardor into the business. When not occupied, and that was during quite a portion of every day, Mr. Hurlburt allowed him free access to the books in the store. Tony often told Mr. Clay, who was his largest customer, that he now found why God had sent him there, instead of into any other kind of employment. It was because he could carry on his education, if he wished, while at the same time he was fulfilling a sacred, present duty.

There was one other visitor to the store over whom Tony endeavored to exert a constant influence, that was his old associate Nick.

Nick had become, in some respects a better boy during Tony's absence from Mountford. Lot's removal from town, and the fact that his father had taken him from school, and kept him constantly occupied under his own eye, had done much to improve him, but the most active and constantly exerted influence for good came from the Sabbath-school. Nick had never left it since the Sabbath Aunt Cily had, so unwillingly to himself, forced him to join her class. He had remained with her as long as she was able to teach, and though he grumbled at first over a change of teachers, still he never left the school, but showed, in his awkward, rough way, an interest in the Bible and good things, which gave some hope for his future to those who cared enough for him to watch these promises with any interest. He tried to come into the book store a few minutes every day, but as there was always some one there Tony had not for many weeks an opportunity for a little private conversation with him, which he so much wished.

At last Nick came in just after dark, when Tony was lighting the swinging lamps, and said, as Mr. Hurlburt had gone away, he thought Tony might be lonely, so he had come with his father's leave, to spend the evening.

Tony was very glad to see him, and in the course of the evening found an opportunity to say,

"Nick, I want to ask you a question, and if you will own up, and tell me the truth, I will promise not to let any living being know that you had the least thing in the world to do with it, I will take the blame all on myself."

Nick started, and felt that he was blushing deeply; what one of all his past sins was going to stare him in the face now; but he said, doggedly, "Go ahead."

"You will answer me then, the truth, the whole truth, and nothing but the truth?"

"Go ahead; if I answer you at all, I shan't tell no lie."

"Very well. Did you send me to steal that melon from old Daddy Lawton?"

Tony fixed his eye steadily on Nick, and saw the color come and go in a manner which assured him at once that his suspicions were just.

"You needn't answer, Nick, I see you did. I have thought that affair over and over a good many times as I grew older, and it always has seemed to me that you and Lot made a cat's paw of me, and because I was such an ignorant little fellow, made me do what you did not dare to. It *was* mean in you, Nick, but I don't intend to blame you for it, you wouldn't do it now, I know you wouldn't, for your right hand, but I tell you what, it's lain on my conscience long enough. I did a great many wicked things with you, but nothing else so bad as thieving. Now I am going to Daddy Lawton to tell him of it, and I am going to pay him for it, and tell him how sorry I am."

"What a big, blundering fool you are," choked out Nick, "the man has forgotten that he ever had that melon; why, bless you, he has raised and sold hundreds as good, or better, since."

"But I have not forgotten it, Nick, nor you either, it seems; now my way is, when I find out I have done wrong, to confess it. I never get over it until I have, and the very name of water-melon, printed in a book, gives me a qualm of conscience I would not go through my life with it for any thing, if I can avoid it."

"Big fool," muttered Nick, indignantly.

"No, I am not a fool, if I were, I should not feel half as sorry as I do now. But, Nick, I am searching for the true wisdom, and that you know is the fear of the Lord. Do you suppose any body can fear God and be a thief?"

"But that was a great while ago."

"Not long enough for me to forget it, and if I have not, why I may be pretty sure God has not;

so Nick, I shall make a clear breast of it before I am twenty-four hours older."

"It's plaguey mean in you."

"Don't call me mean, Nick, it makes the blood tingle all over me. I shall say, and say only, that I took the melon, and if he puts me in the rack (here Tony drew himself up very straight), he won't get any thing more out of me."

Nick seemed a little pacified by this assurance, yet he repeated, "You are a fool, any how."

The next afternoon Tony asked Mr. Hurlburt to spare him an hour or two from the shop, and went, for the first time since the trouting excursion, toward Daddy Lawton's house. He was surprised to see how familiar every thing looked to him as he approached it; but it was in reality no wonder, for Tony had, as he said, many secret misgivings whenever he remembered the melon, which caused him to recall the scene very frequently. He was able to go directly to the spot through which he had crawled under the fence, but it was much too small for him now, though he made an attempt to enter the garden that way.

Daddy Lawton was at home. He sat parching corn by the fire, this being one of his ways of earning a living. He supposed, when he saw Tony, that he was a new customer for the nice, white things, and received him very cordially, giving him at once a handful to test them.

Tony found it much more awkward than he had anticipated to tell the story, but he did it in a very straight forward, manly way, and when he had finished, he put down the amount of money which the melon was worth.

Daddy Lawton interrupted him, as may be supposed, with many exclamations, but ended by saying,

"There wa'ant another such feller in the States, and that if honesty would ever make him President, he was as sure of him as if he was to be inaugurated next fourth of March."

He insisted on not taking the money, and on filling Tony's pockets with the corn; and after many very warm praises, and no fault finding, Tony started, a happier, better boy, on his way home.

Nick came in in the evening to hear the result of the interview, and could not help saying, in a dry kind of way,

"Wa'al now, ra'aly, Tony, honesty is the best policy; how nice these ere corns be, I could not have bought so many for a ninepence, I dare say."

"I dare say not," answered Tony; "but the best of all is, it is off my conscience now, I can look Daddy Lawton in the face, and eat water-melon, too, if I have a fancy, without any twinges of conscience to take away the good taste."

"That's sumthin," added Nick; "I tell you what, Tony, I'll strike a bargain with you, you hold on to me, and kind of keep me up, you know, and I'll promise, just as long as you do, to keep clear of all them plaguey kind of scrapes."

"Agreed," said Tony, cordially extending his hand; and these two boys, although destined to such different paths in life, cemented a friendship which, while it was, as Nick said, the means of keeping him out of much harm, gave Tony great pleasure, for he really loved Nick, and never forgot his generous interference on the day when Lot and Bill so shamefully insulted his aunts.

Here I must leave Nick's career, hoping my readers have felt sufficient interest in him to rejoice that he is in the way of becoming a good, honest, useful man.

Tony's business capacities developed so favorably, that Mr. Hurlburt learned to trust him with much more that is commonly left to boys of his age. He used to send him frequently to the neighboring town to adjust business matters, and on one of these excursions, Mr. Clay gave him a letter, which he asked him to call and deliver to a lad who was at work on a farm, by which he would pass.

Tony read the direction, "Master Horace Atwood." Quite a pretty name, he said to himself; who, pray, can Master Horace be; and what can Mr. Clay want with him; but I don't know as that is any of my business, if it had been, I suppose he would have told me. So Tony went singing and whistling along, driving Mr. Hurlburt's gentle horse, Cato, with much care and most perfect enjoyment. Reaching the farm-house, he tied his pony, and learning from the woman at the door that the boy he was seeking was in the field, he went to find him.

Entering a large potatoe field, he saw a small child very industriously at work picking up potatoes. Going to him, he asked if his name was "Horace Atwood?" and received a very shy "yes," in answer.

"Then, here is a note for you, from Mr. Clay, of Mountford; you know him, I suppose?"

"Yes," said the boy, looking him earnestly in the face, while his own grew very bright, "yes, and I know you, too."

"Know me!" said Tony, in much surprise.

The boy had dropped his hands full of potatoes, and coming close up to Tony, whispered, as if he was afraid the men working at a distance would hear him, "Have you forgotten Poll?"

"Poll, the little circus boy? of course not," said Tony, looking sharply at the round face and red cheeks before him, "do *you* know him?"

"Shouldn't be surprised if I did," said the boy, laughing, "I saw him eat some bread and meat, and cake, that you pushed in through a hole for him once, when he had been flogged, and was half starved to death besides."

"How could that be? I saw no one there but Poll himself."

The boy laughed very merrily, and lifting up his long hair from his cheek, pointed to a deep scar.

"Them's 'um," he said, "he cut deep that time."

Tony was more puzzled than ever, but at last a little light seemed to break upon him."

"*You* are not Poll?" he said.

"Why, not here; I am myself, Horace Atwood, but I was Poll, the circus boy, once."

"And Mr. Clay?" said Tony, drawing the boy so that the sun should fall full upon him.

"Mr. Clay bought me off. You see, there wasn't any body I belonged to, so no one claimed me, and—but I don't know how it was. Mr. Nixon had to let me go, and Mr. Clay brought me here, and I am my own master; I live up there; and there are Ellen and Nancy, and I love them both dearly, so we play together, and I—why I am just the happiest boy in all the world."

"You look very nice," said Tony, rubbing his hands in much delight.

"Oh, I am; I read, and I cipher, and I work on the farm, and Jack and Billy, the two chestnut horses, they know me, as well as the pony did, and they follow me all about every where; beside, I drive them to mill and to meeting, and every where else. Mr. Jenkins, that is the man I live with, says I am first-rate with horses; and I rather guess I am, about middling."

Tony invited Poll, very cordially, to come to

Mountford to see him whenever his master could spare him, and the boy assured him, Mr. Clay had already made him the promise, if he was good and steady, and did not make any trouble, that he would bring him there to spend Christmas and New Years; and, with the hope of soon meeting again, the boys parted.

It is not necessary to follow Tony any further in his upward career. Year after year, as Aunt Roxy came nearer and nearer the end of her pilgrimage, Tony became more support, and a greater earthly comfort. We will have one more look at them in the small house, with which we have become so familiar, before we drop the pen which records the brief history of an orphan child—saved through the mercy of a covenant-keeping God.

It is the day before Christmas, and Tony has been very busy in the book-store, supplying the numerous wants of the customers, who flock in to obtain their Christmas presents. Tony has now reached his sixteenth year, and a finer boy is not to be found in all Mountford. He is above the usual height of youths of his age, with an open, manly face, full of the record of kind. genial, Christian feeling. Mr. Hurlburt feels that his very personal appearance is an advertisement of the strict honesty and honorable dealing which characterize his establishment; and has learned to value him more and more, every year that he has been with him. These years have been years of much mental as well as physical growth to Tony. With free access to the best of books, he has made the most of his time; Mr. Clay has kindly directed and assisted him, and Tony now finds his studies so far advanced, that, could he procure the means, he might enter the last year of the preparatory school in A——, and hope soon to be in college. For this Tony sees no prospect at present; but he has not now to learn to be faithful in attending to the duties of to-day, leaving the morrow in the hands of Him who had so far kindly cared for him. To-day, this day before Christmas, it seemed to him the beautiful gift-books in the store had never looked so temptingly before. There were a few, very dear friends, to whom he would like to present some of them; giving a remembrance, or, rather with him, a token of his gratitude, seemed to be in unison with the spirit of the day. What a gratification it would be, if a few of the dollars he had diligently earned, could be thus appropriated. Tony almost wondered at the tenacity with which the wish clung to him; but, in reality, it was no wonder, for his sale of gifts, of course, constantly brought it to mind. The busy day was at last over, the early shades of the pleasant Christmas eve were falling over the store. Tony, sitting down by the large window, looked out at the different passers by, who were hurrying home.

He saw how many carried boxes, or baskets, or bundles, and Tony had a great deal of pleasure out of them all, for he went home with them, filling the packages with whatever his imagination suggested, and meeting with the pleasant family groups, in this dearest of all home festivals.

As he was very busy in fancy in a pleasant parlor, with the large wicker basket, a man had just carried by, uncovered, and a pretty girl—she had a remarkable resemblance to Alice Clay—hanging the presents it contained, on a beautifully lighted Christmas tree—Mr. Hurlburt called him.

When he went to his desk, he saw, lying upon it, an envelope directed to himself.

"Tony," said Mr. Hurlburt, "you have been with me almost four years, and, so far from having had any occasion to find fault with you, I am free to say, that your services have been of the greatest value to me. I have always been anxious to make you a handsome present, but my affairs have not been heretofore, as you well know, in a condition which would make it right for me to do so. I am now able, and very happy, to give you this Christmas present; not so much as a present, Tony, but to say, that I appreciate the honest, Christian young man, as I always have the honest, Christian boy."

Tony thanked him warmly ; nothing could have been more timely. It seemed to him as if Mr. Hurlburt must have read his thoughts all day, and known how he had been longing for the ability to give those, almost coveted, Christmas gifts.

Very soon he had selected them, and putting them up in neat packages, directed them to those for whom they were designed, before he went home to tea.

Aunt Roxy had lifted the corner of the white window-curtain many times, to look for him, before she hears his well-known footstep on the snow. There is, evidently, some unusual excitement for Aunt Roxy to-night ; something more than the coming Christmas, for she has seen so many of these festivals come and go, in themselves they have become little more than time marks, telling how much nearer she is to the gathering with those who celebrate forever around the throne of the Lamb, the glad birth time of Him their Saviour; but to-night Aunt Roxy has been full of little housekeeping cares; her tottering steps have sounded back and forth —back and forth, many times through the still rooms of her house; something is to happen. *What* can it be? Tony finds everything quiet as usual; indeed, if it had not been, he is so pre-occupied with the unexpected pleasure which he has received, that he would not notice a slight change. Every package is opened, every book shown to Aunt Roxy, whose faded eyes seem almost to rekindle with the light of youth, as she learns from Tony the kind words of appreciation with which Mr. Hurlburt bestowed the gift.

"My precious boy, how very good God is! I will rejoice in the Lord; I will joy in the God of my salvation." And then, Aunt Roxy, with her trembling, quivering voice, as if the joy of her heart could find no other vent but in the way it used long years ago to love so well—the voice of holy song—broke out into the well-known Christmas hymn,

> "While shepherd's watched their flocks by night."

And Tony, with a voice so rich and musical, that it made her feeble tones only the more marked, joined with her; and there they sat, old age and youth, alike in only one thing now, that their hearts beat responsive to the glad strain, that ushered in a world's redemption. In a short time Tony must return to the store; Aunt Roxy asks to have the gift-books left somewhere near her, that they may bear her company while he is gone. And, just before he goes, Tony puts before Aunt Roxy a Bible, with her own name printed in large letters on its envelope; then runs quickly away. But he need not hurry, Aunt Roxy does not stop to open it now; but again commences the series of housekeeping duties. Over and over she dusts the neat rooms, and while she is thus occupied, the back door opens softly, and Alice Clay putting her bright face quite unexpectedly into the parlor, where Aunt Roxy is, asks, in a whisper—

"Has *he* gone! Aunt Roxy?"

"Yes, my pretty lamb; all right, come in."

Then Miss Turner makes her appearance, and —but we must not anticipate. Let us return to Tony.

Mr. Hurlburt is not in the store to-night, and all business ended with the day. Tony hoped Nick would come in to help him to pass the long hours before he could lock up the store, but Nick does not come. Mr. Hurlburt has told him if there was no customers, he might leave an hour earlier to-night, and Tony is not sorry, therefore, when the clock is on the stroke of seven, that there is no one there to prevent his going home. He will take his presents, run with them quickly to the door of those for whom they are designed, then, with as little delay as possible, return to spend the remainder of the evening with Aunt Roxy. Very expeditious Tony is, as he puts the store in perfect order for leaving, and when he at last turns the key in the lock, and feels that he is free for hours, it seems to him the stars were never so bright, nor the air so clear, and full of life and joy. He wonders which of those stars the Star of Bethlehem most nearly resembled, and almost listens, as he walks quickly on, to hear if some strain of the angels' song does not linger yet in the still night air. Tony is very happy to-night, and why should he not be? As he turned the corner of the Methodist church, he stops suddenly—what has happened! Has Aunt Roxy been taken ill? Are the neighbors all in with her? The little house is ablaze with light—up stairs and down—it is almost like an illumination; its small windows stand out like oblong stars on the dark background of the night, and there are lanterns even now, swinging in and out of the back gate. With breathless speed, Tony flies over the remaining distance, bursting into the front door, he finds himself in the midst of nothing more nor less than a small surprise party! There are Mr. and Mrs. Clay, Miss Turner, Nick, with his great red face looking for very joy like a lighted jack-a-lantern. Horace Atwood, no more like Poll than if he had never been the same boy, and quite at home in Tony's little chair, close by Aunt Roxy's side. Mr. and Mrs. White, whom God, in his providence, had returned once more to these scenes of their earlier labors. Mr. Hurlburt, who has brought his wife and four children; and—and—Tony, bewildered and uncertain, cannot quite tell whether the figure standing in the door, with that long kitchen apron on, is an angel or Alice Clay. It has a remarkable resemblance to both, to the boy's excited eye. And then, what a shaking of hands followed; how many wishes for a merry, and a *very* merry Christmas, and how, through it all, Aunt Roxy sat in her old rocking-chair, wiping the tears which would fill her dim eyes, shutting out the room, the company, and even her "own boy."

It was sometime before Tony could see that there was a table in the middle of the room; and, by some magic, the Christmas-tree, which had been floating before him out in the coming twilight, had been transplanted to his own home, and was there blooming in the very centre of the parlor. He saw his own packages, with the large clerk's directions, among them; and now, for the first time, a suspicion crosses his mind, that what was so much of a surprise to him was not to Aunt Roxy, and perhaps it had something to do with her desire to have him leave those books at home, instead of taking them back, as it would have been so much more convenient, to the store.

Nick was too impatient to wait for any one else upon whom it more properly devolved, to explain the scene to Tony. "You see, Tony," he said, "we thought we wanted to keep this night somehow, that would be right pleasant to you, cause—" here Nick choked off rather suddenly—"I mean—cause—cause, we wanted to.

So Mrs. Clay, she got it up—this surprise party, and we all brought our presents. Aunt Roxy knew it all the time. Didn't she keep it slick? I tell you, if she aint about the only woman, I ever saw, that was up to it—I mean to not blabbing the whole thing. Now, my mother, she couldn't no more have done it, than nothing. I say, Aunt Roxy's a brick, now, aint she, Tony?"

Aunt Roxy looked up and smiled, not very much like "a brick" to be sure; but every one knew Nick was not eloquent, so it did not matter; and Tony soon learned from others, that the party had been in contemplation for some time, partly as a reward to him for the quiet, persevering, self-denying manner in which he had adhered to his business, for the last four years, and partly, to show Aunt Roxy, that though she was no longer able to be abroad among them, as she once was, she was not forgotten. The number of friends invited had been purposely kept small, for fear of bringing too much excitement and fatigue upon her, and for that reason they should remain but a short time. But the hours slipped by so pleasantly, that much later than they had designed, they gathered around the Christmas-tree. Tony felt so delighted, that he had a share in the gifts; he was going to thank Mr. Hurlburt again, for having enabled him so to do, when that gentleman took him a moment aside, and said:

"Tony, when you came home to tea, I saw you had entered your books at the retail price; I thought you had been too long in the business not to know that was not the way we sold to dealers, or I should have spoken before; however, as I knew of this surprise-party, and you did not, I took the money which was your due, and bought with it some more little gifts, for those whom you did not expect to meet here to-night. I thought it would be more agreeable to you than any thing else."

It is needless to say how agreeable it was to Tony, and that his gratitude freely expressed, made this a very happy Christmas night to kind Mr. Hurlburt.

Alice was to cut down the presents, and Tony stood ready to lend her his aid, when there were some hanging too far above the reach of those dainty little fingers. Tony hardly knew what or for whom they were, the whole scene was still to him a glimpse into fairy land, too beautiful to be real. At last Mr. Clay recalled him most successfully by putting into his hands an envelope directed to himself, which he told him to open, and read aloud. Tony obeyed. It ran as follows:

"MR. CLAY, DEAR SIR,—I am happy to inform you that the scholarship, for which you applied some time ago, is now vacant; and that upon your recommendation the trustees have voted to offer it to your young friend, Anthony Starr. The money received will meet all but his personal expenses. I hope, both for your sake and his own, the youth may prove himself worthy of the advantages which it offers. The term commences next week on Wednesday.

By order of the Trustees of —— Academy,

RUEBEN LORD, *Secretary.*

JOHN CLAY, ESQ."

The letter dropped from Tony's hand. So suddenly this hope of years granted; the education which had beckoned to him, no matter in what he had been engaged; which he had so longed and prayed for, had come at last. Tony did not think how unselfishly he had sacrificed all these hopes and wishes; how cheerfully and manfully he had accepted other duties when they, and not this, seemed to be in the line of God's appointment; he only felt stunned by the great good which had fallen upon him. It was like the illusion of a dream; he hardly dared to stir, for fear he should waken, and find it gone. But there were too many congratulations to be offered to allow him long to remain in doubt; and when he fully realized all it meant, his first thought, as usual, was not of himself, but of Aunt Roxy.

Aunt Roxy held out both arms to him. "God's blessing on you, my darling," she said, feebly; "never fear for me; when I am old and gray-headed, we know, Tony, dear, who it is that never forsakes us, never, *never*."

"And I am to come and live here," said Miss Turner, cheerfully. "I have done with teaching, Tony; my little scholars have all grown up and left me, and I am too old now, to attach myself to any new faces; so we have it all arranged; Mrs. Clay, Aunt Roxy, and I, and I am to come as soon as you go."

"And she will talk to me of you, Tony," said Aunt Roxy, "and we shall remember what a naughty little boy you were, and how you ran away,"—Aunt Roxy was making a great effort to speak cheerfully, and not to seem cast down—"and how you would not mind, and, oh dear! a great deal that will make us glad such a naughty boy has gone away."

"And I will tell them, Tony," said Mr. Clay, "how that same naughty little boy, God saved through the means of his dead mother's legacy; and how, having found the 'fear of the Lord which is the beginning of wisdom,' he has gone now to garner up earthly wisdom, that he may make a strong pillar in the temple of his God; and that those who hear of the good, which it may perhaps be his privilege to do in future life, shall take courage, and learn new lessons of trust in a covenant-keeping God."

And now it is Alice's turn. Alice, who is always and everywhere sunshine; she dances in, wipes away the tears from the dear old lady's eyes, and putting the trembling hand into her strong young arm, she leads her out to appear to preside over the table, well filled with Christmas dainties, which is spread in the neat kitchen. And then Father White thanks God for the blessings of to-night; thanks him for the mercies and trials of the past; thanks him for the blessed memory of the young mother, who went home so many years ago; and he asks that the blessings she invoked on her orphan boy, may all be heard and answered; and that when the day comes, in which they shall be here no more to spend the glad Christmas, they may all meet, where "partings never come."

THE END.

CPSIA information can be obtained
at www.ICGtesting.com
Printed in the USA
LVHW100028150522
718525LV00007B/56

9 783375 003258